ı this
BOꞁ ıte

Margaret Atwood's books have been published in over thirty-five countries. She is the author of more than forty works of fiction, poetry, critical essays, and books for children. Her novels include *The Handmaid's Tale*, *Cat's Eye*, *The Robber Bride*, *Alias Grace*, which won the Giller Prize in Canada and the Premio Mondello in Italy; *The Blind Assassin*, winner of the 2000 Booker Prize; and *Oryx and Crake*. Margaret Atwood lives in Toronto with writer Graeme Gibson. They are the joint Honourary Presidents of the Rare Bird Club of BirdLife International.

ALSO BY MARGARET ATWOOD

Novels

The Edible Woman

Surfacing

Lady Oracle

Life Before Man

The Handmaid's Tale

Cat's Eye

The Robber Bride

Alias Grace

The Blind Assassin

Oryx and Crake

The Penelopiad

Short Stories

Dancing Girls

Murder in the Dark

Bluebeard's Egg

Wilderness Tips

Good Bones

Good Bones and Simple Murders

The Tent

Moral Disorder

Poetry

Double Persephone

The Circle Game

Speeches for Doctor Frankenstein

The Animals in That Country

The Journals of Susanna Moodie

Procedures for Underground

Power Politics

You Are Happy

Selected Poems (1976)

Two-Headed Poems

True Stories

Interlunar

Selected Poems II: Poems Selected and New 1976–1986

Morning in the Burned House

Non-Fiction

Survival: A Thematic Guide to Canadian Literature

Days of the Rebels 1815–1840

Strange Things: The Malevolent North in Canadian Literature

Negotiating with the Dead: A Writer on Writing

Moving Targets: Writing with Intent: 1982–2004

MARGARET ATWOOD

Bodily Harm

VINTAGE BOOKS
London

FOR JENNIFER RANKIN, 1941–1979.
FOR GRAEME, JAMES AND JOHN.

ACKNOWLEDGEMENTS

The author would like to thank the Canada Council and the Guggenheim Foundation for making it easier to complete this book. She would also like to thank Nan Talese, Donya Peroff, Phoebe Larmore, Michael Bradley, Jennifer Glossop, Jack McClelland, Carolyn Moulton, Rosalie Abella, Dan Green, Susan Milmoe, Carolyn Forché, and the others who are not named but whose help has been essential.

A man's presence suggests what he is capable of doing to you or for you. By contrast, a woman's presence . . . defines what can and cannot be done to her.

John Berger, *Ways of Seeing*

I

T his is how I got here, says Rennie.

It was the day after Jake left. I walked back to the house around five. I'd been over at the market and I was carrying the shopping basket as well as my purse. There wasn't as much to carry now that Jake wasn't there any more, which was just as well because the muscles in my left shoulder were aching, I hadn't been keeping up the exercises. The trees along the street had turned and the leaves were falling onto the sidewalk, yellow and brown, and I was thinking, Well, it's not so bad, I'm still alive.

My next-door neighbour, an old Chinese man whose name I didn't know, was tidying up his front yard. The yard in front of my house had been covered over with paving stones so you could park a car on it. That meant the street was going up rather than down, and in a few years I'd have to move; though I'd stopped thinking in years. My neighbour had pulled up the dead plants and was raking the earth into a raised oblong. In the spring he'd plant things I didn't know the names for. I remember thinking it was time I learned the names, if I was going to live there.

I did notice the cruiser, which they'd left beside a meter like any other car, no flashing lights, but it was a few doors away so I didn't pay much attention to it. You see more police cars down there than you might farther north.

The front door was open, which wasn't out of place on such a warm day. The downstairs neighbour, an old woman who isn't the landlady but behaves like one, has cats and likes to leave the outside door ajar so they can get in and go through the cat door. "Cat hole," Jake calls it; used to call it.

My own door at the top of the stairs was open too. There were people inside, men, I could hear them talking, and then a laugh. I couldn't think who it could be, it wasn't Jake, but whoever it was didn't seem to care who knew they were there. The key was under the mat where I always leave it, but the edge of the doorframe was splintered, the lock was shoved right out of it. I went into the livingroom, which was still piled with the boxes of books Jake had packed but not collected. Nothing had been moved. Through the kitchen doorway I could see feet and legs, shining feet, pressed legs.

Two policemen were sitting at the table. I had that quick rush of fear, late for school, caught on the boys' stairs, caught out. The only thing I could think of was that they were after the pot, but there were no drawers pulled open and the tea and coffee canisters were where they should be. Then I remembered that Jake had taken the whole stash with him. Why not? It was his. Anyway, surely they'd stopped worrying about that, everyone does it now, even the police, it's almost legal.

The younger one stood up, the older one didn't. He stayed sitting down, smiling up at me as if I'd come for a job interview.

You Miss Wilford? he asked. He didn't wait. You're damn lucky. He had a massive head, with the hair clipped short like a punker's. His was left over though, from sometime in the fifties: no green highlights.

Why? I said. What's the matter?

You've got good neighbours, the younger one said. He looked like a high-school gym teacher or a Baptist, about twenty-two, earnest and severe. The one downstairs. She was the one who phoned.

Was it a fire? I said. There was no sign of it, no smell.

The older one laughed. The other one didn't. No, he said. She heard footsteps up here and she knew it wasn't you, she saw you go out, and she didn't hear anyone go up the stairs. He jimmied open your kitchen window.

I put the shopping basket on the table; then I went and looked at the window, which was open about two feet. The white paint was scratched.

You could do it with a jackknife, he said. You should get those safety locks. He heard us coming and went back out through the window.

Did he take anything? I said.

You'll have to tell us that, said the older one.

The younger one looked uneasy. We don't think he was a burglar, he said. He made himself a cup of Ovaltine. He was just waiting for you, I guess. There was a cup on the table, half full of something light brown. I felt sick: someone I didn't know had been in my kitchen, opening my refrigerator and my cupboards, humming to himself maybe, as if he lived there; as if he was an intimate.

What for? I said.

The older one stood up. He took up a lot of space in the kitchen. Take a look, he said, pleased with himself, in charge. He had a present he'd been saving up. He walked past me into the livingroom and then into the bedroom. I was glad I'd made the bed that morning: lately I hadn't always.

There was a length of rope coiled neatly on the quilt. It wasn't any special kind of rope, there was nothing lurid about it. It was off-white and medium thick. It could have been a clothesline.

All I could think of was a game we used to play, Detective or Clue, something like that. You had to guess three things: Mr. Green, in the conservatory, with a pipewrench; Miss Plum, in the kitchen, with a knife. Only I couldn't remember

13

whether the name in the envelope was supposed to be the murderer's or the victim's. *Miss Wilford, in the bedroom, with a rope.*

He was just waiting for you, the younger one said behind me.

Drinking his Ovaltine, the big one said. He smiled down at me, watching my face, almost delighted, like an adult who's just said *I told you so* to some rash child with a skinned knee.

So you were lucky, the younger one said. He came past me and picked up the rope, carefully, as if it had germs. I could see now that he was older than I'd thought, he had anxious puckers around the eyes.

The big one opened the closet door, casually, as if he had every right. Two of Jake's suits were still hanging there.

You live alone, that right? the big one said.

I said yes.

These your pictures? said the big one, grinning.

No, I said. They belong to a friend of mine. The pictures were Jake's, he was supposed to take them away.

Quite a friend, said the big one.

He must've been watching you for a while, said the young one. He must've known when you'd get home. Any idea who it might be?

No, I said. I wanted to sit down. I thought of asking them if they wanted a beer.

Some nut, the big one said. If you knew what was walking around loose out there you'd never go out. You close the curtains in the bathroom when you take a shower?

There aren't any curtains in the bathroom, I said. There aren't any windows.

You close the curtains when you get dressed at night?

Yes, I said.

He'll be back, the young one said. That kind always comes back.

The big one wouldn't let up. You have men over here a lot? Different men?

He wanted it to be my fault, just a little, some indiscretion, some provocation. Next he would start lecturing me about locks, about living alone, about safety.

I close the curtains, I said. I don't have men over. I turn out the lights. I get undressed by myself, in the dark.

The big one smirked at me, he knew about single women, and suddenly I was angry. I unbuttoned my blouse and pulled my left arm out of the sleeve and dropped the slip strap over my shoulder.

What in hell are you doing? the big one said.

I want you to believe me, I said.

●

There's a two-hour stopover in Barbados, or so they tell her. Rennie finds the women's washroom in the new Muzak-slick airport and changes from her heavy clothes to a cotton dress. She examines her face in the mirror, checking for signs. In fact she looks quite well, she looks normal. Her dress is a washed-out blue, her face isn't too pale, she wears only enough makeup so she won't seem peculiar, a leftover hippie or a Plymouth Brethren or something like that. This is the effect she aims for, neutrality; she needs it for her work, as she used to tell Jake. Invisibility.

Take a chance, said Jake, during one of his campaigns to alter her, what was it that time? Purple satin with rhinestone spaghetti straps. Make a statement.

Other people make statements, she said. I just write them down.

That's a cop-out, said Jake. If you've got it, flaunt it.

Which God knows you do, said Rennie.

You're putting me down again, said Jake, affable, showing his teeth, flawless except for the long canines.

You're impossible to put down, said Rennie. That's why I love you.

In the washroom there's a blow-dryer for your hands, which claims to be a protection against disease. The instructions are in French as well as English, it's made in Canada. Rennie washes her hands and dries them under the blow-dryer. She's all in favour of protection against disease.

She thinks about what's behind her, what she cancelled or didn't bother to cancel. As for the apartment, she just shut the door with its shiny new lock and walked out, since out was where she needed to be. It gets easier and easier, dishes in the sink for two weeks, three weeks, only a little mould on them, she hardly even feels guilty any more; one of these days it may be permanent.

Rennie's lucky that she can manage these sidesteps, these small absences from real life; most people can't. She's not tied down, which is an advantage. It's a good thing she's versatile, and it helps to know people, in this case Keith. Keith has recently come across to *Visor* from *Toronto Life*. He's a contact of hers, which is not the same as a friend. While she was in the hospital she decided that most of her friends were really just contacts.

I want to go somewhere warm and very far away, she said.

Try the Courtyard Café, he said.

No, seriously, said Rennie. My life is in the pits right now. I need a tan.

Want to do The Restless Caribbean? he said. So does everyone else.

Nothing political, she said. I can do you a good Fun in the Sun, with the wine lists and the tennis courts, I know what you like.

You finked out on the last piece I wanted you to do, said Keith. Anyway, you just came back from Mexico.

That was last year, she said. Come on, we're old buddies. I need some time out.

Keith sighed and then agreed, a little too quickly. Usually he haggled more. He must have heard about the operation;

maybe he even knew about Jake leaving. He had that faint sick look in his eyes, as if he wanted to give her something, charity for instance. Rennie hates charity.

It's not a total freebie, she said. It's not as if I don't produce.

Pick an island, he said. Only it has to be someplace we haven't done. How about this one? A friend of mine went there, sort of by mistake. He says it's off the beaten track.

Rennie had never heard of it. Sounds great, she said. Ordinarily she would have done some homework, but she was in too much of a hurry. This time she's flying blind.

Rennie repacks her bag, stuffing her pantyhose into an outside pocket, the one with the clock. Then she goes to the restaurant, where everything is wicker, and orders a gin and tonic. She does not look long at the distant sea, which is too blue to be believable.

The restaurant isn't full. There are a few women alone and more in clutches, and a couple of families. There are no men by themselves. Men by themselves usually go to the bar. She knows, she's learned since Jake left, that if she spends much time gazing around the room with that slightly defiant stare adopted by women alone to indicate that they don't have to be, one of the other solitaries might join her. So instead she watches her hands and the ice cubes in her glass, which despite the air conditioning are melting almost at once.

When she goes to the gate she's told the plane is late. Lugging her bag and her camera bag, she walks among the kiosk shops: small black hand-sewn dolls, cigarette boxes and mirrors encrusted with shells, necklaces made from the teeth of sharks, porcupine fish, inflated and dried. A miniature five-piece steel band, mounted on a slab of driftwood, in which the players are toads. Looking more closely, she sees that the toads are real ones that have been stuffed and varnished. A long time ago she would have bought this monstrosity and sent it to someone for a joke.

●

Rennie is from Griswold, Ontario. Griswold is what they call her background. Though it's less like a background, a backdrop – picturesque red Victorian houses and autumn trees on a hillside in the distance – then a subground, something that can't be seen but is nevertheless there, full of gritty old rocks and buried stumps, worms and bones; nothing you'd want to go into. Those who'd lately been clamouring for roots had never seen a root up close, Rennie used to say. She had, and she'd rather be some other part of the plant.

In an earlier phase, Rennie used to tell jokes about Griswold to amuse her friends. Such as: How many people from Griswold does it take to change a lightbulb? The whole town. One to change it, ten to snoop, and the rest of them to discuss how sinful you are for wanting more light. Or: How many people from Griswold does it take to change a lightbulb? None. If the light goes out it's the will of God, and who are you to complain?

People from bigger places, Jake in particular, think that Griswold has an exotic and primitive charm. Rennie doesn't think this. Mostly she tries to avoid thinking about Griswold at all. Griswold, she hopes, is merely something she defines herself against.

Though it's not always so easy to get rid of Griswold. For instance: When Rennie saw the piece of rope on her bed, she knew what Griswold would have had to say about it. This is what happens to women like you. What can you expect, you deserve it. In Griswold everyone gets what they deserve. In Griswold everyone deserves the worst.

The night before the operation Jake took Rennie out to dinner, to cheer her up. She didn't feel like going, but she knew she had been boring recently and she'd vowed, a long time ago, when she was still in her early twenties, never to be boring; a vow that had been harder to keep than she'd expected.

Rennie was an expert on boredom, having done a piece on it for *Pandora*'s "Relationships" column in which she claimed that there were two people involved in boredom, not just one: the borer and the boree. Out-and-out boredom of the jaw-stiffening kind could be avoided by small shifts in attention. *Study his tie,* she recommended. *If you're stuck, make an imaginary earlobe collection and add his. Watch his Adam's apple move up and down. Keep smiling.* The assumption was that the active principle, the source of the powerful ergs of boredom, was male, and that the passive recipient was female. Of course this was unfair, but who except women would read a *Pandora* "Relationships" column? When writing for male-oriented magazines such as *Crusoe* or *Visor* she offered self-help hints: "How To Read Her Mind." *If she's looking too hard at your earlobes or watching your Adam's apple go up and down, change the subject.*

Jake took her to Fentons, which used to be more than he could afford, and they sat under one of the indoor trees. At first he held her hand, but she felt he was doing it because he thought he ought to and after a while he stopped. He ordered a bottle of wine and urged her to drink more of it than she wanted to. Perhaps he thought she would be less boring if she got drunk, but this was not the case.

She didn't want to talk about the operation but she couldn't think about anything else. Maybe it would turn out to be benign; on the other hand, maybe they would open her up and find that she was permeated, riddled, rotting away from the inside. There was a good chance she'd wake up minus a breast. She knew she ought to be thinking about how to die with dignity but she didn't want to die with dignity. She didn't want to die at all.

Jake told stories about people they knew, gossipy stories with a malicious twist, the kind she used to enjoy. She tried to enjoy them but instead she started to think about Jake's fingers: he was holding the stem of his wineglass with his left hand, lightly, but the knuckles were absolutely white. He had a habit of never throwing out empty containers; that morning she'd taken down the Shreddies box and there was nothing in it. How could she know when it was time to get more if he kept leaving empty peanut butter jars and honey jars and cocoa tins on the shelves: she refrained from mentioning this. She felt that Jake's eyes kept slipping away from her face, down to the top button of her blouse; then, as if he'd reached a line, a taboo, back up to her face again. He's fascinated, she thought.

They walked home with their arms around each other, as if they were still in love. While Jake took a shower, Rennie stood in the bedroom with the closet door open, wondering what she should put on. Two of her nightgowns, the black one with the see-through lace top and the red satin one slit up the sides, had been presents from Jake. He liked buying her things like that. Bad taste. Garters, merry widows, red bikini pants with gold spangles, wired half-cup hooker brassieres that squeezed and pushed up the breasts. The real you, he'd say, with irony and hope. Who'd ever guess? Black leather and whips, that's next.

She wanted to make it easy for him, she wanted to help him along with the illusion that nothing bad had happened to her or was going to happen. Her body was in the mirror, looking the same as ever. She couldn't believe that in a week, a day, some of it might have vanished. She thought about what they did with the parts.

In the end she wore nothing. She waited in bed for Jake to come out of the shower. He would smell of body shampoo and he would be damp and slippery. She used to like it when he slid into her wet like that, but tonight she was only waiting for a certain amount of time to be over, as if she were in a dentist's office, waiting for something to be done to her. A procedure.

At first he couldn't. It had been too sudden; she'd been told, she'd told him, the operation had been scheduled, all in the same day. She could understand his shock and disgust and the effort he was making not to reveal them, since she felt the same way. She wanted to tell him he didn't have to, not if it was too much of an effort, but he wouldn't take that well, he'd think she was being critical.

He ran his hand over her breast a couple of times, the bad one. Then he began to cry. This was what she'd been afraid she herself would do. She hugged him, stroking the back of his head.

After that he made love to her, painfully and for a long time. She could hear his teeth grinding together, as if he were angry. He was holding back, waiting for her to come. He thought he was doing her a favour. He was doing her a favour. She couldn't stand the idea of anyone doing her a favour. Her body was nerveless, slack, as if she was already under the anaesthetic. As though he could sense this he gathered skin and muscle, wrenching, twisting, he bit her, not gently, shoving himself into her, trying to break through that barrier of deadened flesh. At last she faked it. That was another vow she'd made once: never to fake it.

●

By the time the flight is called it's already dark. They stand at the gate, a dozen or so of them, watching the plane land. The gate isn't even a gate but an opening in the cement wall with a chain across it. The airline officials, two kids, a light-brown girl who looks about sixteen and a boy with a set of earphones, can't decide which gate they should be standing at, so the whole group straggles back and forth several times between one hole in the wall and another. A man in tinted glasses offers to carry her camera bag for her, but Rennie refuses politely. She doesn't want anyone sitting beside her on the plane, especially a man who would wear a safari jacket. She didn't like safari jackets even when they were still possible. He's the only white man in the group.

When the hole is finally unchained, Rennie follows the others towards the plane, which is tiny and looks alarmingly homemade. Rennie tells herself that you stand a better chance in a small plane like this than a jumbo jet. Jake has a joke about planes. He says they can't really fly, it's absurd to think a heavy piece of metal like that can fly; what keeps them up is the irrational belief of the passengers, and all plane crashes can be explained by a loss of faith.

He'd have a job with this one, she thinks, anyone can see it'll never get off the ground. St. Antoine isn't a rich country, they probably buy their planes fourth-hand from other countries, then stick them together with Band-Aids and string until they fall apart irreparably. It's like the fat trade in restaurants. Rennie knows a lot about the fat trade in restaurants: the good ones selling their used fat to the second-rate ones, and so on down the line until the fat reaches the chipworks of cheap hamburger stands. Rennie's piece on the fat trade was called, "By Their Fats Ye Shall Know Them." The editor's title, not hers. She wanted to call it "Fat City."

She climbs the wobbling metal steps through the dark heat, which is doubled by the heat of the plane. The camera bag strap cuts into her shoulder and the flesh above her left breast; the scar is pulling again. When it feels like this she's afraid to look down, she's afraid she'll see blood, leakage, her stuffing coming out. It isn't a very big scar as such things go; worse thing happen to other people. She's lucky. Why then doesn't she feel lucky?

I don't want to have the operation, she said. She believed two

22

things at once: that there was nothing wrong with her and that she was doomed anyway, so why waste the time? She had a horror of someone, anyone, putting a knife into her and cutting some of her off, which was what it amounted to no matter what they called it. She disliked the idea of being buried one piece at a time instead of all at once, it was too much like those women they were always finding strewn about ravines or scattered here and there in green garbage bags. Dead but not molested. The first time she'd seen that word, in a Toronto newspaper when she was eight, she'd thought a molester was someone who caught moles. A molester is someone who is indecent, said her grandmother. But since that was what her grandmother said about almost everyone, it wasn't much help. Rennie still used that word sometimes, for fun, where other people would use *gross*.

Daniel, who at that point was still Dr. Luoma, looked at her as if he was disappointed in her: other women no doubt said similar things. This embarrassed her, since even such a short time ago she still assumed she was unique.

You don't have to, he said. Or, well, you don't *have* to do anything. Nobody's forcing you, it's your own decision. He paused here, letting her remember that the alternative he offered her was death. *Either/or*. Multiple choice: which was not what it said.

●

During the morning of the day on which she had her routine once-a-year appointment at the gynecologist's, Rennie was working on a piece about drain-chain jewellery. You could get it for pennies at your local Woolworth's, she wrote. Buy as many lengths as you need, make the chains as long as you like with those cunning little peanut-shaped connectors, wear them on any part of your anatomy: wrists, neck, waist, even ankles, if you wanted the slave-girl effect. It was the latest Queen Street thing, she wrote, a New Wave sleaze put-on of real jewellery. Or beyond New Wave even: *nouveau wavé*.

In fact it wasn't the latest Queen Street thing. It wasn't a thing at all, it was an embellishment Rennie had spotted on one of her friends, Jocasta, who ran Ripped Off, a second-hand store on Peter Street that specialized in violently ugly clothes from the fifties, springolator pumps, tiger-stripe pedal pushers, formals with jutting tits and layers of spangles and tulle.

Jocasta was five foot nine, with the cheekbones of an ex-model. She went in for fake leopard-skin shortie coats. The women who hung out at Ripped Off were half Jocasta's age and wore a lot of black leather. They had hair dyed green or bright red, or they shaved their heads with an Iroquois fringe running down the middle. Some of them had safety pins in their ears. They looked up to Jocasta, who was right over the edge in the creative sleaze line and could carry it off, too. In her display window she made arrangements that she called Junk Punk: a stuffed lizard copulating with a mink collar in a child's rocking chair, motorized, a cairn of false teeth with a born-again tract propped against it: "How Can I Be Saved?" Once she hung a coat tree with blown-up condoms sprayed with red enamel and a sign: NATIONAL LOVE A REFUGEE WEEK.

Of course it's gross, said Jocasta. But so's the world, you know what I mean? Me, I'm relaxed. A little deep breathing, mantras of one syllable, bran for breakfast. Can I help it if I'm the wave of the future?

Jocasta wasn't Jocasta's name: her real name was Joanne. She changed it when she was thirty-eight because, as she said, what can you do with a name like Joanne? Too *nice*. She didn't dye her hair green or wear a safety pin in her ear but calling herself Jocasta was the equivalent. Good taste kills, said Jocasta.

Rennie met Jocasta when she was doing a piece on the Queen Street renaissance for *Toronto Life*, all about the conversion of hardware stores and wholesale fabric outlets into French restaurants and trendy boutiques. She did not necessarily believe that a trendy boutique was any improvement over a wholesale fabric outlet, but she knew enough to avoid such negative value judgements in print. At first she thought Jocasta was a lesbian, because of the way she dressed, but later she decided Jocasta was merely bizarre. Rennie liked Jocasta because Jocasta was much more bizarre than Rennie felt she herself could ever be. Partly she admired this quality, partly she felt it was dangerous, and partly, being from Griswold after all, she had a certain contempt for it.

Jocasta wore drain chains because she was miserly and they were cheap. She hadn't even bought her chains, she'd raided the sinks of neighbouring restaurants for them: "All I did was take the plug of with a pair of pliers, and *voilà*." But sometimes Rennie liked to write pieces about trends that didn't really exist, to see if she could make them exist by writing about them. Six to one she'd see at least ten women with bathplug chains looped around their necks two weeks after the piece came out. Successes of this kind gave her an odd pleasure, half gleeful, half sour: people would do anything not to be thought outmoded.

Usually her articles on fake trends were just as plausible as the ones on real trends; sometimes more so, because she tried harder with them. Even the editors were taken in, and when they weren't they'd go along anyway, half-believing that what Rennie had to say on subjects like this would eventually come true, even if it wasn't true at the moment. When she wasn't fooling around she was uncanny, they told each other: as if she could see into the future.

If I could see into the future, Rennie said to one of them (a man, who kept suggesting that they should have drinks sometime soon), do you think I'd waste my time on this sort of thing? The colour of women's lipstick, the length of their skirts, the height of their heels, what bits of plastic or gilt junk they chose to stick on themselves? I see into the present, that's all. Surfaces. There's not a whole lot to it.

Rennie became a quick expert on surfaces when she first moved away from Griswold. (On a university scholarship: the only other respectable way out of Griswold for a young single woman, she used to say, is straight down.) Surfaces determined whether or not people took you seriously, and what was mandatory in Griswold was, more often than not, ludicrous in the real world. Griswold, for instance, was an early convert to polyester knit.

At first she'd looked in order to copy; later on she'd looked in order not to copy. After that she just looked. When Marxist college professors and hard-line feminists gave her a rough time at parties about the frivolity of her subject matter she would counter with a quote from Oscar Wilde to the effect that only superficial people were not concerned with appearances. Then she would tactfully suggest certain alterations to their wardrobes that would improve their own appearances no end. They were usually vain enough to be interested: nobody wanted to be in bad taste.

Most of the people she knew thought Rennie was way out ahead of it, but she saw herself as off to the side. She preferred it there; she'd noted, many times, the typical pose of performers, celebrities, in magazine shots and publicity stills and especially on stage. Teeth bared in an ingratiating smile, arms flung wide to the sides, hands open to show that there were no concealed weapons, head thrown back, throat bared to the knife; an offering, an exposure. She felt no envy towards them. In fact she found them embarrassing, their eagerness, their desperation, for that was what it was, even when they were successful. Underneath it they would do anything; they'd take their clothes off if there was no other way, they'd stand on their heads, anything, in that frenzied grab for attention. She would much rather be the one who wrote things about people like this than be the one that got written about.

Rennie finished the first draft of her piece on drain-chain jewellery and spent some time thinking about the title. Eventually she discarded "The Chain Gang" in favour of "Chain Reaction". The pictures would be easy to get, but she'd leave that to the magazine. She never shot high-gloss fashion, she wasn't good enough.

At eleven-thirty Jake surprised her by coming home, "for a lunchtime quickie," he said. That was fine, since she liked being surprised by him. At that time he was still inventive. Sometimes he would climb up the fire escape and in through the window instead of coming through the door, he'd send her ungrammatical and obscene letters composed of words snipped from newspapers, purporting to be from crazy men, he'd hide in closets and spring out at her, pretending to be a lurker. Apart from the first shock, none of these things had ever alarmed her.

So they had the lunchtime quickie and afterwards Rennie made grilled cheese sandwiches and they ate them in bed, which wasn't as pleasant as she'd thought it would be because some of the crumbs and melted cheese got on the sheets, and Jake went back to his office. Rennie had a bath, because her background was still with her and she felt it would be inconsiderate to go to the gynecologist right after making love without having had a bath.

Ready to have babies yet? The doctor asked, his standard opening joke as he snapped on his prophylactic gloves. You're heading for the cutoff point. He'd been saying this for six years. Half an hour later, everything ceased to be funny.

Though as she walked home she was still thinking in the way she was used to. For instance, she could do a piece on it. "Cancer, The Coming Thing." *Homemakers* might take it, or *Chatelaine*. How about "The Cutoff Point"?

This is a fact, it's happened to you, and right now you can't believe it, she would begin. *You've been used to thinking of yourself as a person, but all of a sudden you're just a statistic* Dying was in bad taste, no doubt of that. But at some point it would be a trend, among the people she knew. Maybe she was way out ahead on that one too.

●

On the plane they serve warm ginger ale in paper cups and sandwiches wrapped in plastic film. The sandwiches are made of slices of white bread, with slightly rancid butter and a thin piece of roast beef between them. Rennie picks out the lettuce: she's been to Mexico, she knows about amoebic dysentery.

The seats are hard and covered with scratchy maroon plush, like those on ancient buses. The stewardesses, two of them, one with straightened upswept hair like Betty Grable's, one with cornrows and beaded Rasta braids, wear hot-pink satin outfits with tiny white aprons. They teeter up and down the narrow aisles on high-heeled sandals, open-toed with multiple straps, magenta: fuck-me shoes, Jake would call them. When the plane bumps they grab for the back of the nearest seat, but they seem used to it.

Though the plane is just half full, there's a man beside Rennie. It isn't the white man in the safari jacket, who's sitting at the very front reading a newspaper, but an older man, brown. He's wearing a dark suit, despite the heat, and a tie in which a small pin shines. She notices that he's taken only one bite of his sandwich. When the remains of the sandwiches are being collected he speaks to Rennie, throwing his voice above the drone of the engines.

"You are from Canada," he says, stating it rather than asking. He's about sixty, spare-faced and tall, with a high-bridged nose; he looks vaguely Arabian. His jaw is undershot, his bottom teeth close slightly over the top ones.

"How did you know?" says Rennie.

"We get mostly Canadians," he says. "The sweet Canadians."

Rennie can't tell whether or not this is meant as irony. "We're not all that sweet," she says.

"I trained in Ontario, my friend," he says. "I was once a veterinarian. My specialty was the diseases of sheep. So I am familiar with the sweet Canadians." He smiles, speaking precisely. "They are famous for their good will. When we had our hurricane, the sweet Canadians donated a thousand tins of ham, Maple Leaf Premium. It was for the refugees." He laughs, as if this is a joke, but Rennie doesn't get it. "The refugees never see this ham," he says, explaining patiently. "Most likely they never eat ham in their lives before. Well, they miss their chance." He laughs again. "The ham turn up, surprise, at the Independence Day banquet. To celebrate our freedom from Britain. For the leading citizens only. Many of us were very amused, my friend. There was a round of applause for the sweet Canadians."

Rennie doesn't know what to say to this. She feels he's making fun of her in some obscure way, but she isn't sure why. "Was it a bad hurricane?" she says. "Was anyone killed?"

He ignores this question entirely. "Why are you coming to St. Antoine?" he says, as if it's an odd thing to be doing.

"I'm writing a piece on it," she says. "A travel piece."

"Ah," he says. "To entice the sweet Canadians."

Rennie is becoming irritated with him. She looks at the pocket in the seatback in front of her, hoping there's something she can pretend to read, an airline magazine, barf-bag mags as they're known in the trade, but there's nothing in it but the card illustrating emergency procedures. On the 707 to Barbadoes she had a thriller she bought at the airport, but she finished it and left it on the plane. A mistake: now she's bookless.

"You must visit our Botanic Gardens," he says. "The British made very good ones, all over the world. For medicinal purposes, you understand. Ours is one of the oldest. It is still in good repair; they have only been gone a month. Now that we are free, we have to pull out the weeds ourselves. We have a small museum there, you must see that. Broken pots made by the Carib Indians and so forth. They did not make very accomplished pottery. We still have a few of them in our country, we have not fully modernized."

He reaches into his jacket pocket and takes out a bottle of aspirin. He taps two into his palm and offers the bottle to Rennie, as if offering a cigarette. Rennie doesn't have a headache, but feels she should take one anyway, it's the polite thing to do.

"There is a fort also," he says. "The British were proficient at that, too. Fort Industry. Under the British it was called Fort George, but our government is renaming everything." He signals the stewardess and asks for a glass of water.

"We just have ginger ale," she says.

"It will have to do," he says. His teeth clamp together in a bulldog grin. "In my country that is a very useful phrase."

The ginger ale comes and he swallows his aspirins, then offers the styrofoam cup to Rennie. "Thank you," says Rennie. "I'm saving mine for later." She holds the aspirin in her hand, wondering if she's just been rude, but if so he doesn't seem to notice.

"I have many statistics you might find useful," he says. "Those on unemployment, for instance. Or perhaps you would prefer the Botanic Gardens? I would be happy to escort you, I take an interest in plants."

Rennie decides not to ask him about restaurants and tennis courts. She thanks him and says she'll have a better idea of what she's looking for once she gets there.

"I think we are approaching," he says.

The plane dips. Rennie peers out the window, hoping to see something, but it's too dark. She glimpses an outline, a horizon, something jagged and blacker than the sky, but then the plane goes down at a forty-five degree angle and a moment later they hit the ground. She jolts forward against the seat belt as the plane brakes, much too fast.

"We have a very short runway here," he remarks. "Before I tendered my regrets to the present government I attempted to have something done about it. I was at that time the Minister for Tourism." He smiles his lopsided smile. "But the Prime Minister had other priorities."

The plane taxis to a stop and the aisle jams with people. "It's been nice meeting you," Rennie says as they stand up.

He holds out his hand for her to shake. Rennie transfers the aspirin. "I hope you will have a pleasant stay, my friend. If you need assistance, do not hesitate to call on me. Everyone knows where I can be found. My name is Minnow, Dr. Minnow, like the fish. My enemies make jokes about that! A small fish in a small puddle, they say. It is a corruption of the French, Minôt was the original, it was one of the many things they left behind them. The family were all pirates."

"Really?" Rennie says. "That's wild."

"Wild?" says Dr. Minnow.

"Fascinating," says Rennie.

Dr. Minnow smiles. "They were common once," he says. "Some of them were quite respectable; they intermarried with the British and so forth. You have a husband?"

"Pardon?" says Rennie. The question has caught her by surprise: nobody she knows asks it any more.

"A man," he says. "Here we do not bother so much with the formalities."

Rennie wonders if this is a sexual feeler. She hesitates. "Not *with* me," she says.

"Perhaps he will join you later?" Dr. Minnow says. He looks down at her anxiously, and Rennie sees that this isn't an advance, it's concern. She smiles at him, hoisting her camera bag.

"I'll be fine," she says. Which is not what she believes.

●

When Rennie floated up through the anaesthetic she did not feel anything at first. She opened her eyes and saw light green, then closed them again. She did not want to look down, see how much of herself was missing. She lay with her eyes closed, realizing that she was awake and would rather not be. She also realized, though she had not admitted it before, that she had expected to die during the operation. She'd heard stories about people going into shock or being allergic to the anaesthetic. It was not out of the question.

Her left arm was numb. She tried to move it and couldn't. Instead she moved her right hand, and not until then did she understand that someone was holding it. She turned her head, forced her eyes to open, and saw, a long distance away, as if she were looking through the wrong end of a telescope, the image of a man, a head surrounded by darkness, glassy and clear. Daniel.

It's all right, he said. It was malignant but I think we got it all.

He was telling her that he had saved her life, for the time being anyway, and now he was dragging her back into it, this life that he had saved. By the hand. *Malignant*, Rennie thought.

Now what, she said. Her mouth felt thick and swollen. She looked at his arm, which was bare from the elbow down and was lying beside hers on the white sheet; hair licked along the skin like dark flames. His fingers were around her wrist. She did not see hands but an odd growth, like a plant or something with tentacles, detachable. The hand moved: he was patting her.

Now you go to sleep, he said. I'll be back.

Rennie looked again and his hand attached itself to his arm, which was part of him. He wasn't very far away. She fell in love with him because he was the first thing she saw after her life had been saved. This was the only explanation she could think of. She wished, later, when she was no longer feeling dizzy but was sitting up, trying to ignore the little sucking tubes that were coming out of her and the constant ache, that it had been a potted begonia or a stuffed rabbit, some safe bedside object. Jake sent her roses but by then it was too late.

I imprinted on him, she thought; like a duckling, like a baby chick. She knew about imprinting; once, when she was hard up for cash, she'd done a profile for *Owl Magazine* of a man who believed geese should be used as a safe and loyal substitute for watchdogs. It was best to be there yourself when the goslings came out of the eggs, he said. Then they'd follow you to the ends of the earth. Rennie had smirked because the man seemed to think that being followed to the ends of the earth by a flock of adoring geese was both desirable and romantic, but she'd written it all down in his own words.

Now she was behaving like a goose, and the whole thing put her in a foul temper. It was inappropriate to have fallen in love with Daniel, who had no distinguishing features that Rennie could see. She hardly even knew what he looked like, since, during the examinations before the operation, she hadn't bothered to look at him. One did not look at doctors; doctors were functionaries, they were what your mother once hoped you would marry, they were fifties, they were passé. It wasn't only inappropriate, it was ridiculous. It was expected. Falling in love with your doctor was something middle-aged married women did, women in the soaps, women in nurse novels and in sex-and-scalpel epics with titles like *Surgery* and nurses with big tits and doctors who looked like Dr. Kildare on the covers. It was the sort of thing *Toronto Life* did stories about, soft-core gossip masquerading as hard-nosed research and exposé. Rennie could not stand being guilty of such a banality.

But there she was, waiting for Daniel to appear (out of nowhere, she never knew when he would be coming, when she was having a sponge bath or struggling to the toilet, leaning on the large wattled nurse), hooked like a junkie on those pats of the hand and Rotarian words of cheer and collective first-person plurals ("We're coming along nicely"), and in a feeble rage because of it. *Shit*. He wasn't even that handsome, now that she had a good look: his proportions were wrong, he was too tall for his shoulders, his hair was too short, his arms were too long, he gangled. She sniffled with anger into the wad of Kleenex the nurse held out to her.

A good cry will do you good, said the nurse. But you're lucky, they say there's none anywhere else, some of them are full of it, they cut it out and it just pops up somewhere else. Rennie thought of toasters.

Daniel brought her a pamphlet called *Mastectomy: Answers to Down-To-Earth Questions*. Down to earth. Who wrote these things? Nobody in her position would want to think very hard about *down* or *earth*. *Are there any restrictions on sexual activity?* she read. The pamphlet suggested that she ask her doctor. She considered doing this.

But she didn't. Instead, she asked him, How much of me did you cut off? Because she was in love with him and he hadn't noticed, her tone of voice was not all it should have been. But he didn't seem to mind.

About a quarter, he said gently.

You make it sound like a pie, said Rennie.

Daniel smiled, indulging her, waiting her out.

I guess I should be relieved, said Rennie. That you didn't hack off the whole thing.

We don't do that any more unless there's massive involvement, said Daniel.

Massive involvement, said Rennie. It's never been my thing.

He follows up, said the nurse. A lot of them, they just do their number and that's that. He likes to know how things work out, in their life and all. He takes a personal interest. He says a lot of it has to do with their attitude, you know?

Jake brought champagne and pâté and kissed her on the

mouth. He sat beside her and tried not to look at her wrapped chest and the tubes. He spread pâté on crackers, which he'd also brought, and fed them to her. He wanted to be thanked.

You're a godsend, she said. The food here is unbelievable. Green Jello salad and a choice of peas or peas. She was happy to see him but she was distracted. She didn't want Daniel to walk in, trailing interns, while Jake was still there.

Jake was restless. He was healthy and healthy people are embarrassed by sickness, she could remember that. She was convinced also that she smelled peculiar, that there was a faint odour of decay seeping through the binding: like an off cheese. She wanted him to go quickly and he wanted to go.

We'll get back to normal, she told herself, though she could not remember any longer what *normal* had been like. She asked the nurse to adjust her bed so she could lie back.

That's a fine young man, the nurse said. Jake was a fine young man. He was all in place, a good dancer who hardly ever bothered to dance.

●

Rennie climbs down the steps of the plane and the heat slips over her face like thick brown velvet. The terminal is a low shed with a single turret. It looks grey under the weak lights of the runway, but as Rennie walks toward it she sees that it's really yellow. Over the doorway there's a bronze plaque thanking the Canadian government for donating it. It's odd to see the Canadian government being thanked for anything.

The immigration officer is wearing a dark-green uniform, like a soldier's, and there are two actual soldiers leaning against the wall beside him, in crisp blue shirts with short sleeves. Rennie assumes they're soldiers, since they have shoulder holsters with what look like real guns in them. They're young, with skinny innocent bodies. One of them is flicking his swagger stick against his pantleg, the other has a small radio which he's holding against his ear.

Rennie realizes she's still clutching the aspirin in her left hand. She wonders what to do with it; somehow she can't just throw it away. She opens her purse to put it with her other aspirins, and the soldier with the swagger stick saunters towards her.

Rennie feels a chill sweep down her. She's about to be singled out: perhaps he thinks the bottle she's holding contains some kind of illegal drug.

"It's aspirin," she says, but all he wants is to sell her a ticket to the St. Antoine Police Benefit Dance, Semi-formal, Proceeds For Sports Funds. So they're only police, not soldiers. Rennie makes this out by reading the ticket, since she hasn't understood a word he's said.

"I don't have the right kind of money," she says.

"We take anything you got," he says, grinning at her, and this time she understands him. She gives him two dollars, then adds a third; possibly it's the price of admission. He thanks her and strolls back to the other one, and they laugh together. They haven't bothered with anyone else in the line.

In front of Rennie there's a tiny woman, not five feet tall. She's wearing a fake-fur shortie coat and a black wool jockey cap tilted at a rakish angle. She turns around now and looks at up Rennie.

"That a bad man," she says. "Don't you have nothin' to do with that one." She holds out to Rennie a large plastic bag full of cheese puffs. From under the brim of her jockey cap her eyes peer up out of her dark wrinkled face, she must be at least seventy but it's hard to tell. The eyes are bright, candid, sly, the eyes of a wary child.

"This my grandson," she says. She opens the coat to reveal an orange T-shirt. PRINCE OF PEACE, it says in large red letters.

Rennie has never seen a religious maniac up close before. When she was at university an economics student was rumoured to have run through his dormitory one night, claiming to have given birth to the Virgin Mary, but that was put down to pre-exam tension.

Rennie smiles, as naturally as possible. If this woman thinks she's Ste. Anne or whoever, it would be best not to upset her, not in the immigration line at any rate. Rennie accepts some cheese puffs.

"It my grandson, all right," says the woman. She knows she's been doubted.

Then it's her turn, and Rennie hears her say to the immigration officer in a shrill, jocular voice, "You give me trouble, my grandson blaze your arse good for you." This seems to have the desired effect, for the man stamps her passport immediately and she goes through.

When he comes to Rennie he feels he has to be extra severe. He flips through her passport, frowning over the visas. He wears thick bifocals, and he pushes them further down on his nose and holds the passport away from him, as if it smells funny.

"Renata Wilford? That you?"

"Yes," Rennie says.

"It don't look like you."

"It's a bad picture," Rennie says. She knows she's lost weight.

"Let her in, man," one of the policemen calls, but the immigration clerk ignores him. He scowls at her, then at the picture. "What the purpose of your visit?"

"Pardon?" Rennie says. She has to strain to understand the accent. She looks around for Dr. Minnow, but he's nowhere in sight.

"What you doin' here?" He glares at her, his eyes enlarged by the lenses.

"I'm a writer," Rennie says. "A journalist. I write for magazines. I'm doing a travel piece."

The man glances over at the two policemen. "What you goin' to write about here?" he says.

Rennie smiles. "Oh, the usual," she says. "You know, restaurants, sight-seeing, that sort of thing."

The man snorts. "Sight-seein'," he says. "No pretty lights here." He stamps her passport and motions her through.

"Write it good," he says to her as she goes past. Rennie thinks he's teasing, as such a man at Heathrow or Toronto or New York would be. They would say, "Write it good, honey." Or *love*, or *sweetheart*. They would grin. But when she turns to give the required smile he's staring straight ahead, through the plateglass window to the tarmac, where the plane has already turned in the darkness and is taxiing again for take-off between the rows of white and blue lights.

Rennie changes some money, then waits while a tired uniformed woman pokes through her purse and her bags. Rennie says she has nothing to declare. The woman scrawls a chalk mark on each of her bags, and Rennie walks through a doorway into the main room. The first thing she sees is a large sign that says, THE BIONIC COCK. IT GIVES YOU SPURS. There's a picture of a rooster; it turns out to be an advertisement for rum.

There's a crowd outside the door, taxi drivers, and Rennie goes with the first one who touches her arm. Ordinarily she would talk with him, finds things out: beaches, restaurants, shops. But it's too hot. She sinks into the marshmallow-soft upholstery of the car, some derelict from the fifties, while the driver goes far too fast through the winding narrow streets, honking at every bend. The car is on the wrong side of the road, and it takes Rennie a moment to remember that this is in fact the British side.

They wind up a hillside, past houses she can make out only dimly. The headlights shine on massive bushes overhanging the road, with flamboyant red and pink flowers dangling from them like Kleenex flowers at a high-school dance. Then they're in the lighted part of town. There are crowds of people on the streetcorners and in front of the shops but they aren't walking, they're just standing or sitting on steps or chairs, as if they're inside a room. Music flows through the open doorways.

Some of the men wear knitted wool caps, like tea cosies, and Rennie wonders how they can stand it in the heat. Their heads turn as the taxi goes by, and some wave and shout, at the driver rather than Rennie. She's beginning to feel very white. Their blacks aren't the same as our blacks, she reminds herself; then sees that what she means by *our blacks* are the hostile ones in the States, whereas *our blacks* ought to mean this kind. They seem friendly enough.

Nevertheless Rennie finds their aimlessness disturbing, as she would at home. It's too much like teenagers in shopping plazas, it's too much like a mob. She discovers that she's truly no longer *at home*. She is away, she is *out*, which is what she wanted. The difference between this and home isn't so much that she knows nobody as that nobody knows her. In a way she's invisible. In a way she's safe.

●

When Jake moved out, naturally there was a vacuum. Something had to come in to fill it. Maybe the man with the rope hadn't so much broken into her apartment as been sucked in, by the force of gravity. Which was one way of looking at it, thought Rennie.

Once she would have made this man into a good story; she would have told it at lunch, with the strawberry flan. She wasn't sure what stopped her, from telling anyone at all. Perhaps it was that the story had no end, it was open-ended; or perhaps it was too impersonal, she had no picture of the man's face. When she was outside, walking along the street, she looked at the men who passed her in a new way: it could be any one of them, it could be anyone. Also she felt implicated, even though she had done nothing and nothing had been done to her. She had been seen, too intimately, her face blurred and distorted, damaged, owned in some way she couldn't define. It wasn't something she could talk about at lunch. Anyway, she didn't want to become known as a man-hater, which was what happened when you told stories like that.

The first thing she did after the policemen had gone was to get the lock fixed. Then she had safety catches put on the windows. Still, she couldn't shake the feeling that she was being watched, even when she was in a room by herself, with the curtains closed. She had the sense that someone had been in her apartment while she was out, not disarranging anything, but just looking into her cupboards, her refrigerator, studying her. The rooms smelled different after she'd been out. She began to see herself from the outside, as if she was a moving target in someone else's binoculars. She could even hear the silent commentary: Now she's opening the bean sprouts, now she's cooking an omelette, now she's eating it, now she's washing off the plate. Now she's sitting down in the livingroom, nothing much going on. Now she's getting up, she's going into the bedroom, she's taking off her shoes, she's turning out the light. Next comes the good part.

She began to have nightmares, she woke up sweating. Once she thought there was someone in the bed with her, she could feel an arm, a leg.

Rennie decided she was being silly and possibly neurotic as well. She didn't want to turn into the sort of woman who was afraid of men. It's your own fear of death, she told herself. That's what any armchair shrink would tell you. You think you're dying, even though you've been saved. You should be grateful, you should be serene and profound, but instead you're projecting onto some pathetic weirdo who's never going to bother you again. That scratching you heard at the window last night wasn't coming from the outside at all.

Which was all very well, but the man existed; he was an accident that had almost happened to her; he was an ambassador, from some place she didn't want to know any more about. The piece of rope, which was evidence, which the police had taken away with them, was also a message; it was someone's twisted idea of love. Every time she went into her bedroom she could see it, coiled on the bed, even though it was no longer there.

In itself it was neutral, and useful too, you could use it for all kinds of things. She wondered whether he'd intended to strangle her with it or just tie her up. He hadn't wanted to be drunk, there had been beer and half a bottle of wine in the refrigerator, she was sure he'd looked, and he'd chosen Ovaltine. He'd wanted to know what he was doing. When he got as far as the scar perhaps he would have stopped, apologized, untied her, gone home, to the wife and children Rennie was certain he had. Or perhaps he knew, perhaps that's what turned him on. *Mr X. in the bedroom, with a rope.*

And when you pulled on the rope, which after all reached down into darkness, what would come up? What was at the end, *the end*? A hand, then an arm, a shoulder, and finally a face. At the end of the rope there was someone. Everyone had a face, there was no such thing as a faceless stranger.

●

Rennie is late for dinner. She has to wait at the front desk while they set a table for her in the diningroom. Around the corner, where she can't see, a tray of silverware hits the floor and there's an argument in low voices. After fifteen minutes a waitress comes out and says sternly that Rennie can go in now, as if it's a trial rather than a meal.

As Rennie walks towards the diningroom, a woman with a tan the colour of clear tea walks out of it. She has blonde hair braided and wound around her head, and she's wearing a sleeveless magenta dress with orange flowers on it. Rennie feels bleached.

The woman smiles at her with fluorescent teeth, looking at her with round blue china-doll eyes. "Hi there," she says. Her friendly, glassy stare reminds Rennie of the greeting perfected by hostesses in the restaurants of Holiday Inns. Rennie waits for her to say, "Have a good day." The smile lasts a little too long, and Rennie gropes, wondering if she knows this woman. She decides with relief that she doesn't, and smiles back.

The tables are covered with starched white tablecloths and the wineglasses have linen napkins tucked into them, pleated into fans. Propped against the flower vase, one hibiscus per table, is a small typewritten card which isn't exactly a menu, since there's no choice. The food is brought by three waitresses, in light-blue full-skirted dresses and white aprons and mobcaps. They are totally silent and do not smile; perhaps they've been called away from their own dinners.

Rennie begins to compose, from habit and to pass the time, though she doesn't think the Sunset Inn will finds its way into her piece:

The décor is nondescript, resembling nothing so much as an English provincial hotel, with flowered wallpaper and a few prints of hunting and shooting. The ceiling fans add a pleasant touch. We began with the local bread, and butter of perhaps a questionable freshness. Then came (she consulted the menu) *a pumpkin soup, which was not the bland version most North Americans may be used to. My companion . . .*

But there is no companion. It's necessary to have a companion for these excursions, always, if only a paper one. The readers would find the suggestion that you would go to a restaurant and sit there all by yourself, just eating, far too depressing. They want gaiety and the possibility of romance and a mention of the wine list.

Rennie gives up anyway when the roast beef arrives, leathery and khaki and covered with a gravy that tastes like mix. It's garnished with a cube of yam and something light green that has been boiled too long. This is the kind of food you eat only when very hungry.

Rennie is reminded of the put-on piece she did, months ago, on fast-food outlets. It was for *Pandora*'s "Swinging Toronto" section. She'd once done a piece for them on how to pick men up in laundromats, unobtrusively and safely, with addresses of the good laundromats. *Check their socks. If they ask to borrow your soap flakes, forget it.*The food franchise piece was called "Sawdust Yummies" and the subtitle (not hers) read, "You better take a good thou, 'cause the bread and the wine are nowhere."

She'd covered every McDonald's and Kentucky Fried Chicken spot in the downtown core for it, dutifully taking one bite of everything. *My companion had the Egg McMuffin, which he found a trifle runny. My buns were chilly.*

Rennie picks at the alien vegetables on her plate, gazing around the room. There's only one other diner, a man, who's sitting on the far side of the room reading a paper. In front of him is a dish of what looks like whipped lime Jello. If this were a laundromat, would she pick him up? He turns the page of his newspaper and smiles at her, a half-smile of complicity, and Rennie looks down at her plate. She likes to stare but she doesn't like to be caught doing it.

Eye contact, that was one hint. She's not surprised when he folds the paper, gets up, and heads towards her table.

"It's kind of dumb, sitting across the room from each other like that," he says. "I think this place is empty except for us. Mind if I join you?"

Rennie says no. She has no intention of picking this man up. She never actually picked men up in laundromats, she just went through the preliminaries and then explained that she was doing research. That's what she can always say if necessary. Meanwhile, there's no reason not to be polite.

He goes to the kitchen door and asks for another cup of coffee, and one of the waitresses brings it. She also brings a dish of the green substance for Rennie, and then, instead of returning to the kitchen, sits down at the man's vacated place and finishes off his dessert, staring balefully at him as she does so. The man has his back to her and can't see.

"I wouldn't eat that if I were you," he says.

Rennie laughs and looks at him more carefully. Before the operation, there was a game she used to play with Jocasta, on the street and in restaurants. Pick a man, any man, and find the distinguishing features. The eyebrows? The nose? The body? If this man were yours, how would you do him over? A brush cut, a wet suit? It was a rude game and Rennie knew it. Jocasta, for some reason, didn't. Listen, she'd say. You'd be doing them a favour.

Rennie thinks this man would resist being done over. For one thing, he's too old: he's past the Silly Putty stage. Rennie decides he must be at least forty. His tan is leathery, there are permanent white creases around his eyes. He has a light moustache and post-hippie-length hair, bottom of the earlobes in front, top of the collar in back; it's a little ragged, as if he does it himself with kitchen scissors. He's wearing shorts and a yellow T-shirt without anything written on it. Rennie approves of this. She liked T-shirts with mottoes on them when they first came out, but now she thinks they're jejune.

Rennie introduces herself and mentions that she's a journalist. She always likes to get that in first, before people mistake her for a secretary. The man says his name is Paul and he's from Iowa. "Originally," he says, implying travel. He's not staying at the hotel, he says, just eating there. It's one of the better places.

"If this is better, what's worse?" says Rennie, and they both laugh.

Rennie asks him where home is. It's all right to ask such questions, since Rennie has already decided this does not have the flavour of a pickup. File it under *attempt at human contact*. He just wants someone to talk to, he's killing time. Which is fine, that's all she's doing herself. If there's anything she doesn't need in her life right now, it's another one of what Jocasta would call *those*. Nevertheless, she's conscious of a desire to stick her head down under the tablecloth, to see what his knees look like.

"Home?" says Paul. "You mean, where the heart is?"

"Was that a personal question?" says Rennie. She starts to eat the dessert, which appears to be made of sweetened chalk.

Paul grins. "Most of the time I live on a boat," he says. "Over at Ste. Agathe, the harbour's better there. I'm just here for a couple of days, on business."

Rennie feels she's expected to ask what sort of business, so she doesn't. She's decided he will be boring. She's met people with boats before and all they ever talk about is boats. Boats make her seasick. "What sort of boat?" she says.

"Quite a fast one. Actually I have four of them," he says, watching her. Now she's supposed to be impressed.

"I guess that means you're filthy rich," she says.

This time he laughs. "I charter them out," he says. "They're all out now. It's a pain in the ass in some ways. I don't like tourists. They're always complaining about the food, and they throw up too much."

Rennie, who is a tourist, lets this pass. "How did you get four?" she says.

"You can pick them up cheap around here," he says, "from the dead or the disgusted, retired stockbrokers who have heart attacks or decide it's too much trouble scraping off the barnacles. There's a bit of owner piracy too."

Rennie doesn't want to give him the satisfaction of her ignorance, but he smiles at her with his tan folding into pleats around his eyes, he wants her to ask, so she relents and asks.

"People stealing their own boats," he says. "They collect the insurance. Then they sell the boat."

"But you would never do a thing like that," says Rennie. She's paying more attention. No gold earring, no wooden leg, no hooks on the ends of the arms, no parrot. Still, there's something. She looks at his hands, square-fingered and practical, carpenter's hands, on the tablecloth, not doing anything.

"No," he says. "I would never do a thing like that."

He smiles a little, his eyes are light blue, and she recognizes something about him, a deliberate neutrality. He's doing what she does, he's holding back, and now she's really curious.

"Do you have a job?" she says.

"If you have four boats you don't exactly need a job, around here," he says. "I make enough on the charters. I used to have one, I was an agronomist with the U.S. Department of Agriculture. They sent me as an adviser. I was supposed to be telling them what else they can grow here besides bananas. I was pushing red kidney beans. The catch is, nobody really wants them to grow anything here besides bananas. But they wouldn't send me anywhere else, so I kind of retired."

"Where were you before that?" says Rennie.

"Here and there," he says. "A lot of places. I was in Viet Nam, before the war, the official one that is. After that I was in Cambodia." He says this still smiling, but looking at her straight on, a little belligerently, as if he's expecting her to react, with horror or at least disgust.

"What were you doing there?" says Rennie pleasantly, putting down her spoon.

"Advising," he says. "I was always advising. It's not the same as having people do what you say."

"What about?" says Rennie; she feels now as if they're on the radio.

There's a small pause, another crinkled smile. "Rice," he says, watching her closely.

She's being asked for something, but she's not sure what it is. Not admiration, not absolution. Maybe she's not being asked for anything at all, which is just as well, since she doesn't have a whole lot of handouts left. "That must have been interesting," she says. She hasn't done profiles for nothing, she isn't stupid, she knows how to add, she knows there's an X factor. Ten years ago she would have felt entitled to moral outrage, but it's no skin off her nose. People get trapped in things that are beyond their control, she ought to know that by now.

He relaxes, leans back in his chair. She's passed the test, whatever it is. "I'll tell you about it sometime," he says, assuming the future; which is more than she can do.

●

Rennie's room at the Sunset Inn is papered with a small floral print, pink and blue; there are several pale-orange water-marks near the ceiling, which is fifteen feet high. At the end of the bed, which is single and narrow and covered with a white chenille spread, hangs a picture of a green melon cut open to reveal the seeds. Over the bed itself is a knotted mosquito net, not quite as white as the bedspread. On the night table beside the bed are a Bible, a mosquito coil in a saucer, a box of matches, Three Star, made in Sweden, and a lamp with a pleated paper shade. The lamp is a mermaid with her arms over her head, holding up the bulb. Her breasts aren't bare, she's wearing a harem jacket open at the front, its edges grazing the nipples. In the drawer of the night table are two more mosquito coils in a box labelled *Fish Mosquito Destroyer, Blood Protection Co. Ltd.*

On the pale-green bureau there's a thermos jug of water, a glass and a hand-printed card warning visitors not to drink the tap water. Rennie opens the drawers. In the centre one is a lime-green blanket, in the bottom one a safety pin. Rennie feels momentarily that she may be spending the rest of her life in rooms like this. Not her own.

She lights the mosquito coil, turns on the mermaid lamp and puts her travelling alarm clock on top of the Bible. She unpacks her cotton nightgown and the zipper bag in which she keeps her toothbrush and other pieces of cleaning and sterilizing equipment people use on their bodies. She's ceased to take such things for granted; "Prevention of Decay" is no longer just a slogan. She closes the Venetian blind on the narrow window, turns off the overhead light and undresses. The mirror over the bureau is small, so she isn't reflected anywhere.

She takes a shower, in water that refuses to become more than lukewarm. When she comes out of the tiny bathroom, there's a green lizard sticking to the wall beside the window.

She turns down the chenille spread and the sheet and looks carefully in the bed and under the pillow, checking for wildlife. She untwists the mosquito net and tucks it around the bed. Then she crawls into the white tent, turns off the light, and moves to the centre of the bed so that no part of her body is touching the net. She can see the oblong of the window, grey against the darkness, and the glowing end of the mosquito coil. The air is warm and damp, warmer and damper on her skin now than before she took the shower, and the bed smells faintly of mildew.

There are sounds from outside the window, a high cricket sound and a repeated note like a bell or a waterglass being struck, some kind of insect or frog perhaps, and beyond that the insistent syncopated music. Several minutes after she turns out the light a car backfires, or maybe it's firecrackers, and a woman screams with laughter; but that stops and the music keeps going.

Despite the heat Rennie lies with her arms folded, left hand on her right breast, right hand on the ridge of skin that slants across the side of her breast up towards her armpit. This is how she always sleeps now.

She runs the fingers of her left hand over the skin of her breast, the good one, the one she hopes is good, as she does every night. From the surface you can feel nothing, but she no longer trusts surfaces. She brushed her teeth and cleaned them with dental floss, prevention of decay, and rinsed out her mouth with water from the thermos, which smells like melted ice cubes, like the inside of a refrigerator, like cloth in a truck. Nevertheless she can still taste the airplane sandwich, slightly rancid butter and roast beef, rotting meat.

She sleeps and wakes fitfully, listening to the music and, occasionally, a car going past in what always sounds like the wrong gear. She feels clogged and furry; she's convinced she's been snoring, though it hardly matters. At last she sinks into a heavy damp sleep.

She wakes up suddenly. She can feel something like moist cloth, webbing, pressing down over her eyes and mouth. Her face is against the net. Through it she can see the figures on her digital clock, the dot pulsing like a tiny heart. It's six in the morning. She was dreaming that someone was climbing in through the window.

She remembers where she is and hopes she hasn't bothered anyone in the hotel by screaming. She's too warm, she's sweating, and despite the mosquito net she has several bites, from where she's rolled against the net. The muscles of her left shoulder are aching again.

There's a rooster crowing nearby and beyond that a dog, dogs. The room is growing light. Close to her ear, on the other side of the wall, there are sounds it takes her a moment to recognize, unfamiliar, archaic, the rhythmic creak of a bed and a woman's voice, wordless and mindless. Before she places it she hears it as agony. Once this intrusion would merely have irritated her, or, if she was with someone, amused or even excited her. Now it's painful to her, mournful, something lost, a voice from the past, severed from her and going on beside her in another room. Get it over, she thinks through the wall.

Oh please.

●

II

One of the first things I can remember, says Rennie, is standing in my grandmother's bedroom. The light is coming in through the window, weak yellowish winter light, everything is clean, and I'm cold. I know I've done something wrong, but I can't remember what. I'm crying, I'm holding my grandmother around both legs, but I didn't think of them as legs, I thought of her as one solid piece from the neck down to the bottom of her skirt. I feel as if I'm holding on to the edge of something, safety, if I let go I'll fall, I want forgiveness, but she's prying my hands away finger by finger. She's smiling; she was proud of the fact that she never lost her temper.

I know I will be shut in the cellar by myself. I'm afraid of that, I know what's down there, a single lightbulb which at least they leave on, a cement floor which is always cold, cobwebs, the winter coats hanging on hooks beside the wooden stairs, the furnace. It's the only place in the house that isn't clean. When I was shut in the cellar I always sat on the top stair. Sometimes there were things down there, I could hear them moving around, small things that might get on you and run up your legs. I'm crying because I'm afraid, I can't stop, and even if I hadn't done anything wrong I'd still be put down there, for making a noise, for crying.

Laugh and the world laughs with you, said my grandmother.

Cry and you cry alone. For a long time I hated the smell of damp mittens.

I grew up surrounded by old people: my grandfather and my grandmother, and my great-aunts and great-uncles, who came to visit after church. I thought of my mother as old too. She wasn't, but being around them all the time made her seem old. On the street she walked slowly so they could keep up with her, she raised her voice the way they did, she was anxious about details. She wore clothes like theirs too, dark dresses with high collars and small innocuous patterns, dots or sprigs of flowers.

As a child I learned three things well: how to be quiet, what not to say, and how to look at things without touching them. When I think of that house I think of objects and silences. The silences were almost visible; I pictured them as grey, hanging in the air like smoke. I learned to listen for what wasn't being said, because it was usually more import-ant than what was. My grandmother was the best at silences. According to her, it was bad manners to ask direct questions.

The objects in the house were another form of silence. Clocks, vases, end-tables, cabinets, figurines, cruet sets, cranberry glasses, china plates. They were considered im-portant because they had once belonged to someone else. They were both overpowering and frail: overpowering because threatening. What they threatened you with was their frailty; they were always on the verge of breaking. These objects had to be cleaned and polished once a week, by my grandmother when she was still well enough and after-wards by my mother. It was understood that you could never sell these objects or give them away. The only way you could ever get rid of them was to will them to someone else and then die.

The objects weren't beautiful, most of them. They weren't supposed to be. They were only supposed to be of the right kind: the standard aimed at was not beauty but decency.

That was the word, too, among my mother and my aunts, when they came to visit. "Are you decent?" they would call gaily to one another before opening bedroom or bathroom doors. Decency was having your clothes on, in every way possible.

If you were a girl it was a lot safer to be decent than to be beautiful. If you were a boy, the question didn't arise; the choice was whether or not you were a fool. Clothes could be decent or indecent. Mine were always decent, and they smelled decent too, a wool smell, mothballs and a hint of furniture polish. Other girls, from families considered shoddy and loose, wore questionable clothes and smelled like violets. The opposite of decent wasn't beautiful, but flashy or cheap. Flashy, cheap people drank and smoked, and who knew what else? Everyone knew. In Griswold, everyone knew everything, sooner or later.

So you had your choice, you could decide whether people would respect you or not. It was harder if your family wasn't respectable but it could be done. If your family was respectable, though, you could choose not to disgrace it. The best way to keep from disgracing it was to do nothing unusual.

The respectability of my family came from my grandfather, who had once been the doctor. Not a doctor, the doctor: they had territories then, like tomcats. In the stories my grandmother told me about him, he drove a cutter and team through blizzards to tear babies out through holes he cut in women's stomachs and then sewed up again, he amputated a man's leg with an ordinary saw, knocking the man out with his fist because no one could hold him down and there wasn't enough whisky, he risked his life by walking into a farmhouse where a man had gone crazy and was holding a shotgun on him the whole time, he'd blown the head off one of his children and was threatening to blow the heads off the other ones too. My grandmother blamed the wife, who had run away months before. My grandfather saved the lives of the remaining children, who were then put in an orphanage. No one wanted to adopt children who had such a crazy father and mother: everyone knew such things ran in the blood. The man was sent to what they called the loony bin. When they were being formal they called it an institution.

My grandmother worshipped my grandfather, or so everyone said. When I was little I thought of him as a hero, and I guess he was, he was about the closest you could get in Griswold unless you'd been in the war. I wanted to be like him, but after a few years at school I forgot about that. Men were doctors, women were nurses; men were heroes, and what were women? Women rolled the bandages and that was about all anyone ever said about that.

The stories my mother and aunts told about my grandfather were different, though they never told these stories when my grandfather was there. They were mostly about his violent temper. When they were girls, whenever they skirted what he felt to be the edges of decency, he would threaten to horsewhip them, though he never did. He thought he was lenient because he didn't make his children sit on a bench all Sunday as his own father had. I found it very difficult to connect these stories, or my grandmother's either, with the frail old man who could not be disturbed during his afternoon nap and who had to be protected like the clocks and figurines. My mother and my grandmother tended him the same way they tended me, efficiently and with a lot of attention to dirt; only more cheerfully. Perhaps they really were cheerful. Perhaps it made them cheerful to have him under their control at last. They cried a lot at his funeral.

My grandmother had been amazing for a woman of her age; everyone told me that. But after my grandfather's death she began to deteriorate. That's how my mother would put it when her sisters would come to visit. They were both married, which was how they'd got away from Griswold. I was in high school by then so I didn't spend as much time hanging around the kitchen as I used to, but one day I walked in on them and all three of them were laughing, stifled breathless laughs, as if they were in a church or at a funeral:

they knew they were being sacrilegious and they didn't want my grandmother to hear them. They hardly saw me, they were so intent on their laughter.

She wouldn't give me a key to the house, my mother said. Thought I'd lose it. This started them off again. Last week she finally let me have one, and I dropped it down the hot air register. They patted their eyes, exhausted as if they'd been running.

Foolishness, said my aunt from Winnipeg. This was my grandmother's word for anything she didn't approve of. I'd never seen my mother laugh like that before.

Don't mind us, my aunt said to me.

You laugh or you cry, said my other aunt.

You laugh or you go bats, said my mother, injecting a little guilt, as she always did. This sobered them up. They knew that her life, her absence of a life, was permitting them their own.

After that my grandmother began to lose her sense of balance. She would climb up on chairs and stools to get things down, things that were too heavy for her, and then she would fall. She usually did this when my mother was out, and my mother would return to find her sprawled on the floor, surrounded by broken china.

Then her memory began to go. She would wander around the house at night, opening and shutting doors, trying to find her way back to her room. Sometimes she wouldn't remember who she was or who we were. Once she frightened me badly by coming into the kitchen, in broad daylight, as I was making myself a peanut butter sandwich after school.

My hands, she said. I've left them somewhere and now I can't find them. She was holding her hands in the air, helplessly, as if she couldn't move them.

They're right there, I said. On the ends of your arms.

No, no, she said impatiently. Not those, those are no good any more. My other hands, the ones I had before, the ones I touch things with.

My aunts kept watch on her through the kitchen window while she wandered around in the yard, prowling through the frost-bitten ruins of the garden which my mother didn't have the time to keep up any more. Once it had been filled with flowers, zinnias and scarlet runner beans on poles where the hummingbirds would come. My grandmother once told me heaven would be like that: if you were good enough you would get everlasting life and go to a place where there were always flowers. I think she really believed it. My mother and my aunts didn't believe it, though my mother went to church and when my aunts visited they all sang hymns in the kitchen after supper when they were doing the dishes.

She seems to think it's still there, said my aunt from Winnipeg. Look. She'll freeze to death out there.

Put her in a home, said my other aunt, looking at my mother's caved face, the mauve half-moons under her eyes.

I can't, my mother would say. On some days she's perfectly all right. It would be like killing her.

If I ever get like that, take me out to a field and shoot me, said my other aunt.

All I could think of at that time was how to get away from Griswold. I didn't want to be trapped, like my mother. Although I admired her – everyone was always telling me how admirable she was, she was practically a saint – I didn't want to be like her in any way. I didn't want to have a family or be anyone's mother, ever; I had none of those ambitions. I didn't want to own any objects or inherit any. I didn't want to cope. I didn't want to deteriorate. I used to pray that I wouldn't live long enough to get like my grandmother, and now I guess I won't.

●

Rennie wakes up finally at eight. She lies in bed and listens to the music, which seems to be coming from downstairs now, and decides she feels much better. After a while she gropes her way through the mosquito netting and gets out of bed. She leans on the windowsill, looking out at the sunlight, which is very bright but not yet ferocious. Down below is a cement courtyard, she seems to be at the back of the hotel, where a woman is washing sheets in a zinc tub.

She considers her wardrobe. There isn't much choice, since she packed the minimum.

She remembers picking out the basic functional sunbreak mix 'n' match, wrinkle-free for the most part. That was only the day before yesterday. After she'd packed, she had gone through her cupboard and her bureau drawers, sorting, rearranging, folding, tucking the sleeves of her sweaters carefully behind their backs, as if someone would be staying in her apartment while she was away and she needed to leave things as tidy and manageable as possible. That was only the clothes. The food in the refrigerator she'd disregarded. Whoever it was wouldn't be eating.

Rennie puts on a plain white cotton dress. When the dress is on she looks at herself in the mirror. She still looks normal.

Today she has an appointment with the radiologist at the hospital. Daniel made it for her weeks ago, he wants more tests. A work-up, they call it. She didn't even cancel the appointment before taking off. She knows that later she will regret this lack of courtesy.

Right now she only feels she's escaped. She doesn't want the tests; she doesn't want the tests because she doesn't want the results. Daniel wouldn't have scheduled more tests unless he thought there was something wrong with her again, though he said it was routine. She's in remission, he says. *But we'll have to keep an eye on you, we always will. Remission* is the good word, *terminal* is the bad one. It makes Rennie think of bus stations: the end of the line.

She wonders whether she's already become one of those odd wanderers, the desperate ones, who cannot bear the thought of one more useless hospital ordeal, pain and deathly sickness, the cells bombarded, the skin gone antiseptic, the hair falling out. Will she go off on those weird quests too, extract of apricot pits, meditation on the sun and moon, coffee enemas in Colorado, cocktails made from the juice of cabbages, hope in bottles, the laying on of hands by those who say they can see vibrations flowing out of their fingers in the form of a holy red light? Faith healing. When will she get to the point where she'll try anything? She doesn't want to be considered crazy but she also doesn't want to be considered dead.

Either I'm living or I'm dying, she said to Daniel. Please don't feel you can't tell me. Which is it?

Which does it feel like? said Daniel. He patted her hand. You're not dead yet. You're a lot more alive than many people.

This isn't good enough for Rennie. She wants something definite, the real truth, one way or the other. Then she will know what she should do next. It's this suspension, hanging in a void, this half-life she can't bear. She can't bear not knowing. She doesn't want to know.

She goes into the bathroom, intending to brush her teeth. In the sink there's a centipede, ten inches long at least, with far too many legs, blood-red, and two curved prongs at the back, or is it the front? It's wriggling up the side of the slippery porcelain sink, falling back again, wriggling up, falling back. It looks venomous.

Rennie is unprepared for this. She's not up to squashing it, what would she use anyway? And there's nothing to spray it with. The creature looks far too much like the kind of thing she's been having bad dreams about: the scar on her breast splits open like a diseased fruit and something like this crawls out. She goes into the other room and sits down on the bed, clasping her hands together to keep them from shaking. She waits five minutes, then wills herself back into the bathroom.

The thing is gone. She wonders whether it dropped from the ceiling in the first place, or came up through the drain, and now where has it gone? Over the side onto the floor, into some crack, or back down the drain again? She wishes she had some Drano and a heavy stick. She runs some water into the sink and looks around for the plug. There isn't one.

●

There's a lounge where you can have afternoon tea; it's furnished with dark green leatherette chairs that look as if they've been hoisted from an early-fifties hotel foyer in some place like Belleville. Rennie waits on one of the sticky chairs while they set a table for her in the diningroom, grudgingly, since she's half an hour late. In addition to the chairs there's a glass-topped coffee table with wrought-iron legs on which there are copies of *Time* and *Newsweek* eight months old, and a mottled plant. Gold tinsel is looped around the tops of the windows, left over from Christmas; or perhaps they never take it down.

The tablecloths from the night before have been removed; underneath, the tables are grey formica with a pattern of small red squares. Instead of the pleated linen fans there are yellow paper napkins. Rennie looks around for Paul but there's no sign of him. The hotel seems fuller, though. There's an older woman, white, thin-faced, by herself, who stares perkily around the diningroom as if expecting to be charmed by everything, and an Indian family, the wife and grandmother in saris, the little girls in frilled sundresses. Luckily, Rennie is placed one table away from the older woman, who looks unpleasantly Canadian. She doesn't want to have a conversation about scenery or the weather. The three little girls parade the room, giggling, being chased and pinched playfully by the two waitresses, who smile for them in a way they do not smile for adults.

The older woman is joined by another like herself, plumper

but with hair as tight. Listening to them, watching them consult their little books, Rennie discovers that they aren't Canadian but German: one of that army of earnest travellers that is everywhere now on the strength of the Deutschmark, even in Toronto, blue-eyed, alert, cataloguing the world. Why not? thinks Rennie. It's their turn.

The waitress comes and Rennie orders yoghurt and fresh fruit.

"No fresh fruit," says the waitress.

"I'll take the yoghurt anyway," says Rennie, who feels she's in need of some friendly bacteria.

"No yoghurt," says the waitress.

"Why is it on the menu then?" says Rennie.

The waitress looks at her, straight-faced but with her eyes narrowing as if she's about to smile. "Used to be yoghurt," she says.

"When will there be some again?" Rennie says, not sure why this should all be so complicated.

"They got Pioneer Industries for dairy now," the waitress says, as if reciting a lesson. "Government thing. Dairy don't make no yoghurt. Yoghurt need powder milk. Powder milk outlaw, you can't buy it. The yoghurt place shut down now."

Rennie feels that there are connections missing here, but it's too early in the morning to have to deal with this. "What can I have then?" she says.

"What we got," says the waitress, very patiently.

This turns out to be orange juice made from instant powder of some sort, an almost-cooked egg, coffee from a jar with tinned milk, bread with margarine, and guava jelly, too sweet, dark orange, of the consistency of ear wax. Rennie wishes she could stop reviewing the food and just eat it. Anyway, she isn't at the Sunset Inn because of the food. She's here because of the price: this time the deal isn't all-expenses. She can do the other, flossier places for lunch or dinner.

The waitress comes and takes away her plate, the runny egg in its custard cup, the pieces of bread and jam lying beside it. Like a child, she's eaten the centres and left the crusts.

After breakfast comes the rest of the day, which will surely be too long, too hot and bright, to be filled with any activity that will require movement. She wants to go to sleep in the sun on a beach, but she's prudent, she doesn't want to come out like crispy chicken. She needs suntan lotion and a hat. After that she can start going through the motions: places of interest, things to do, tennis courts, notable hotels and restaurants, if any.

She knows you become exhausted in the tropics, you lose momentum, you become comatose and demoralized. The main thing is to keep going. She has to convince herself that if she doesn't manage to complete a well-researched and cheerfully written piece on the pleasures of St. Antoine the universe will be negatively affected.

Maybe she could fake the whole article, concoct a few ravishing little restaurants, some Old World charm in the New World, throw in some romantic history, tart the whole thing up with a few photos from the lesser-known corners of, say, St. Kitts. She pictures legions of businessmen descending on St. Antoine and then, in outrage, on the editorial offices of *Visor*. It won't do, she'll have to come up with something, she's overdrawn at the bank. She can always talk about development potential.

What I need is a pith helmet, she thinks, and some bearers, or are they beaters, to carry me around in a hammock, and some of what those people in Somerset Maugham are always drinking. Pink gin?

●

Rennie does what she does because she's good at it, or that's what she says at parties. Also because she doesn't know how to do anything else, which she doesn't say. Once she had ambitions, which she now thinks of as illusions: she believed

63

there was a right man, not several and not almost right, and she believed there was a real story, not several and not almost real. But that was 1970 and she was in college. It was easy to believe such things then. She decided to specialize in abuses; honesty would be her policy. She did a piece for the *Varsity* on blockbusting as practised by city developers and another on the lack of good day-care centres for single mothers, and she took the nasty and sometimes threatening letters she received as a tribute to her effectiveness.

Then she graduated and it was no longer 1970. Several editors pointed out to her that she could write what she liked, there was no law against it, but no one was under any obligation to pay her for doing it, either. One of them told her she was still a southern Ontario Baptist at heart. United Church, she said, but it hurt.

Instead of writing about the issues, she began interviewing the people who were involved in them. Those pieces were a lot easier to sell. The *in* wardrobe for the picket line, the importance of the denim overall, what the feminists eat for breakfast. The editors told her she was better at that anyway. Radical chic, they called it. One day she found herself short of petty cash and did a quick piece on the return of hats with veils. It wasn't even radical, it was only chic, and she tried not to feel too guilty about it.

Now that she no longer suffers from illusions, Rennie views her kind of honesty less as a virtue than a perversion, one from which she still suffers, true; but, like psoriasis and hemorrhoids, those other diseases typical of Griswold, it can be kept under control. Why make such things public? Her closet honesty is – there's no doubt about it – a professional liability.

Other people have no such scruples. Everything is relative, everything is fashion. When a thing or a person has been too widely praised, you merely reverse the adjectives. No one considers this perverse, it's simply the nature of the business, and the business runs on high turnover. You write about something until people become tired of reading about it or you become tired of writing about it, and if you're good enough or lucky enough it's the same thing. Then you write about something else.

Rennie is still close enough to Griswold to find this attitude irritating at times. Last year she went into the office of the *Toronto Star* when some of the younger staff members were making up a list. It was close to New Year's and they were drinking gallon white wine out of styrofoam coffee cups and killing themselves laughing. The list was a regular feature. Sometimes it was called "In and Out," sometimes "Plus and Minus"; such lists reassured people, including those who wrote them. It made them think they could make distinctions, choices that would somehow vindicate them. She had once composed such lists herself.

This time the list was called "Class: Who Has It, Who Doesn't." Ronald Reagan didn't have class, Pierre Trudeau did. Jogging didn't have class, contemporary dance did, but only if you did it in jogging pants, which did, for that but not for jogging, but not in stretchy plunge-back leotards, which didn't for that but did if you went swimming in them, instead of in bathing suits with built-in bra cups, which didn't. Marilyn's didn't, the Lickin' Chicken on Bloor, which didn't sell chicken, did.

"What else for the No list?" they asked her, giggling already, anticipating her answer. "What about Margaret Trudeau?"

"What about the word *class*?" she said, and they weren't sure whether that was funny or not.

Which is a problem she has. The other problem is the reputation she's getting for being too picky. She's aware of this, she listens to gossip; people are beginning to think she won't finish assignments. There's some truth to this: increasingly there are things she can't seem to do. Maybe it isn't *can't*, maybe it's *won't*. What she wants is something legitimate to say. Which is childish. Loss of nerve, she's decided. It started before the operation but it's getting worse. Maybe she's having a mid-life crisis, way too soon. Maybe it's Griswold squeezing her head: *If you can't say anything nice, don't say anything at all.* Not that its own maxims ever stopped Griswold.

Two months ago she was offered a good piece, a profile in *Pandora*'s "Women of Achievement" series. A ballet dancer, a poet, a female executive from a cheese food company, a judge, a designer who specialized in shoes with glitter faces on the toes. Rennie wanted the designer but they gave her the judge, because the judge was supposed to be hard to do and Rennie was supposed to be good.

Rennie was not prepared for the panic that overtook her the first day out. The judge was nice enough, but what did you say? What does it feel like to be a judge? she asked. What does it feel like to be anything? said the judge, who was only a year older than Rennie. She smiled. It's a job. I love it.

The judge had two wonderful children and an adoring husband who didn't at all mind the time she spent being a judge, because he found his own job so satisfying and rewarding. They had a charming house, Rennie couldn't fault the house, filled with paintings by promising young artists; the judge decided to be photographed in front of one of them. With each question Rennie felt younger, dumber and more helpless. The judge had it all together and Rennie was beginning to see this as a personal affront.

I can't do it, she told the editor at *Pandora*. The editor's name was Tippy; she was a contact of Rennie's. She opens her mouth and out comes this ticker tape.

She's a control freak, Tippy said. She's controlling the interview. You've got to turn it around, get an angle on her. Our readers want them to be human too, a few cracks in the armour, a little pain. Didn't she have to suffer on her way up?

I asked her that, said Rennie. She didn't.

What you have to do, said Tippy, is ask her if you can just

sort of hang out with her. Follow her around all day. There's a real story in there somewhere. How she fell in love with her husband, did you ask that? Look in the medicine cabinet, go for the small details, it matters what they roll on under their arms, Arrid or Love, it makes a difference. Stick with them long enough and sooner or later they crack. You've got to dig. You're not after dirt, just the real story.

Rennie looked across the desk, which was messy, at Tippy, who was also messy. She was ten years older than Rennie, her skin was sallow and unhealthy, there were pouches under her eyes. She chain-smoked and drank too much coffee. She was wearing green, the wrong colour for her. She was a good journalist, she'd won all sorts of awards before she became an editor, and now she was telling Rennie to peer into other people's medicine cabinets. A woman of achievement.

Rennie went home. She looked at what she'd already written about the judge and decided that it was, after all, the real story. She tore it up and started a new page.

A profile used to mean a picture of somebody's nose seen from the side, she wrote. *Now it means the picture of somebody's nose seen from the bottom.* Which was as far as she got.

●

Rennie takes her camera, on the off chance. She's not very good, she knows that, but she forced herself to learn because she knew it would increase her scope. If you do both the pictures and the text you can go almost anywhere, or so they say.

She picks up a mimeographed map of Queenstown and a tourist brochure from the registration desk. "St. Antoine and Ste. Agathe," the brochure says. "Discover Our Twin Islands In The Sun." On the front is a tanned white woman laughing on a beach, sheathed in one-piece aqua Spandex with a modesty panel across the front. A black man in a huge straw hat is sitting on the sand beside her, handing her up a coconut with a couple of straws sticking out of it. Behind him is a machete propped against a tree. He's looking at her, she's looking at the camera.

"When was this printed?" Rennie asks.

"We get them from the Department of Tourism," says the woman behind the desk. "That's the only kind there is." She's British and seems to be the manager, or perhaps the owner. Rennie is always slightly cowed by women like this, women who can wear thick-soled khaki shoes and lime-green polyester jersey skirts without being aware of their ugliness. This woman's no doubt responsible for the lounge chairs and the scabby plant. Rennie envies people who are unaware of ugliness: it gives them an advantage, they can't be embarrassed.

"I understand you're a travel writer," the woman says severely. "We don't usually have them here. You ought to be at the Driftwood."

For a moment Rennie wonders how she knows, but then remembers that it says "freelance journalist" on her disembarkation card, which is in the office safe. Not a hard deduction. What she probably means is that Rennie can't expect special treatment because there isn't any, and in particular she's not supposed to ask for a discount.

The hotel is on the second floor of an old building. Rennie goes down the outside stone staircase, the steps worn concave in the centres, to an inner courtyard that smells of piss and gasoline, then under an archway into the street. Sunlight hits her like a wind, and she rummages in her purse for sunglasses. She realizes she's stepped over a pair of legs, trousers with bare feet at the ends, but she doesn't look down. If you look they want something. She walks along beside the wall of the hotel, patchy stucco that was once white. At the corner she crosses the main street, which is pocked with holes; thick brown sludge moves in the gutters. There aren't many cars. On the other side of the street is an overhang supported by columns, a colonnade, like the ones bordering the *zócalos* in Mexican towns. It's hard to tell how old things are, she'll have to find out. The tourist brochure says the Spaniards were through here, once, along with everyone else. "Leaving a charming touch of Old Spain" is how they put it.

She walks in the shade, looking for a drugstore. Nobody bothers her or even looks at her much, except for a small boy who tries to sell her some spotty bananas. This is a relief. In Mexico, whenever she left Jake at the hotel and ventured out by herself, she was followed by men who made sucking noises at her with their mouths. She buys a straw hat, over-priced, in a shop that sells batiks and shellwork necklaces made from the vertebrae of fish. It also sells bags, and because of that it's called Bagatelle. Not bad, thinks Rennie. There are familiar signs: The Bank of Nova Scotia, The Canadian Imperial Bank of Commerce. The bank buildings are new, the buildings surrounding them are old.

In the Bank of Nova Scotia she cashes a traveller's cheque. A couple of doors down there's a drugstore, also new-looking, and she goes into it and asks for some suntan lotion.

"We have Quaaludes," the man says as she's paying for the lotion.

"Pardon?" says Rennie.

"Any amount," the man says. He's a short man with a gambler's moustache, balding, his pink sleeves rolled to the elbows. "You need no prescription. Take it back to the states," he says, looking at her slyly. "Make you a little money."

Well, it's a drugstore, Rennie thinks. It sells drugs. Why be surprised? "No thank you," she says. "Not today."

"You want the hard stuff?" the man asks.

Rennie buys some insect repellent, which he rings up halfheartedly on the cash register. Already he's lost interest in her.

●

Rennie walks uphill, to the Church of St. Antoine. It's the oldest one left, says the tourist brochure. There's a graveyard surrounding it, the plots enclosed by wrought-iron fences, the gravestones tipping and overgrown with vines. On the lawn there's a family planning poster: KEEP YOUR FAMILY THE RIGHT SIZE. No hints about what that might be. Beside it is another poster: ELLIS IS KING. There's a picture of a fattish man, smiling like a Buddha. It's been defaced with red paint.

Inside, the church is completely empty. It feels Catholic, though there are no squat guttering red candles. Rennie thinks of the Virgins in Mexico, several of them in each church, dressed in red or white or blue or black; you chose one and prayed to it according to your needs. Black was for loss. The skirts of the Virgins had been studded with little tin images, tin arms, tin legs, tin children, tin sheep and cows, even tin pigs, in thanks for what had been restored, or perhaps only in hope that it might be. She'd found the idea quaint, then.

There's an altar at the front, a table at the back with a slotted box where you can buy postcards, and a large picture on the west wall, "by an early unknown local artist," says the brochure. It's St. Anthony, being tempted in the desert; only the desert is bursting with tropical vegetation, vivid succulent red flowers, smooth flat leaves bulging with sap, brightly coloured birds with huge beaks and yellow eyes, and St. Anthony is black. The demons are noticeably paler, and most of them are female. St Anthony is on his knees in an attitude of prayer, his eyes turned up and away from the scaly thighs, the breasts and pointed scarlet tongues of the demons.

He isn't wearing one of those bedspreads she remembers from the Griswold Sunday school handouts but an ordinary shirt, white and open at the throat, and brown pants. His feet are bare. The figures are flat, as if they've been cut from paper, and they cast no shadows.

There are postcards of the painting on the table, and Rennie buys three. She has her notebook with her but she doesn't write anything in it. Then she sits down in the back pew. What part of herself would she pin on the skirt of the black Virgin now, if she had the chance?

Jake went to Mexico with her. It was their first trip together. He didn't like the churches much: churches didn't do a whole lot for him, they reminded him of Christians. Christians have funny eyes, he said. Clean-minded. They're always thinking about how you'd look as a bar of soap.

I'm one, said Rennie, to tease him.

No, you're not, said Jake. Christians don't have cunts. You're only a *shiksa*. That's different.

Want to hear me sing "Washed in the Blood of the Lamb"? said Rennie.

Don't be perverted, said Jake. You're turning me on.

Turning? said Rennie. I thought you were on all the time.

It was a whole week. They were euphoric, they held hands on the street, they made love in the afternoons, the wooden louvres of the old windows closed against the sun, they got flea bites, there was nothing that didn't amuse them, they bought dubious cakes and strange fried objects from roadside stands, they ate them recklessly, why not? They found a sign in a little park that read, *Those found sitting improperly in the park will be punished by the authorities.* It can't mean that, said Rennie. We must've translated it wrong. What is *sitting improperly*? They walked through the crowded streets at night, curious, fearless. Once there was a fiesta, and a man ran past them with a wickerwork cage balanced on his head, shooting off rockets and Catherine wheels. It's you, Rennie said. Mr. General Electric.

She loved Jake, she loved everything. She felt she was walking inside a charmed circle: nothing could touch her, nothing could touch them. Nevertheless, even then, she could feel the circle diminishing. In Griswold they believed that everything evened out in the end: if you had too much good luck one day, you'd have bad the next. Good luck was unlucky.

Still, Rennie refused to feel guilty about anything, not even the beggars, the women wrapped in filthy *rebozos*, with the fallen-in cheeks of those who have lost teeth, suckling inert babies, not even brushing the flies away from their heads, their hands held out, for hours on end it seemed, in one position as if carved. She remembered stories she'd heard about people who mutilated themselves and even their children to make tourists feel sorry for them; or was that in India?

At the end of the week Jake got a case of Montezuma's Revenge. Rennie bought a bottle of sweet pink emulsion for him at the corner *farmacia*, running the gauntlet of sucking mouths, and he allowed himself to be dosed. But he wouldn't lie down. He didn't want her to go anywhere without him, he didn't want to miss anything. He sat in a chair, clutching his belly and limping to the bathroom at intervals, while Rennie consulted him about her piece. "Mexico City On Less Than You'd Think."

I'm supposed to be doing this other piece too, she said, for *Pandora*. It's on male pain. How about it? What's the difference?

Male what? Jake said, grinning. You know men don't feel pain. Only when they cut themselves shaving.

It's just been discovered that they do, she said. Tests have been done. Papers have been presented. They wince. Sometimes they flinch. If it's really bad they knit their brows. Come on, be a nice guy, give me a few hints. Tell me about male pain. Where do you feel it the most?

In the ass, Jake said, during conversations like this. Enough with the instant insight.

It's a living, she said, it keeps me off the streets. Where would I be without it? You wouldn't feel so much pain in the ass if you'd take the poker out.

That's not a poker, it's a backbone, he said. I got it from pretending to be a *goy*. Girls can never tell the difference.

Only between the backbone and the front bone, she said. She sat down on his lap, one leg on either side of him, and began to lick his ear.

Have a heart, he said, I'm a sick man.

Beg for mercy, she said. Do boys cry? We have ways of making you talk. She licked his other ear. You're never too sick, she said. She undid the buttons on his shirt and slid her hand inside it. Anyone as furry as you could never be too sick.

Enough with the voracious female animalistic desires, he said. You should all be locked in cages.

He put his arms around her and they rocked slowly back and forth, and outside the wooden shutters a bell rang somewhere.

●

Rennie walks back on the shadow side. After a few blocks she realizes she's not entirely sure where she is. But she came up to get to the church, so now all she has to do is head down, towards the harbour. Already she's coming to some shops.

Someone touches her on the shoulder, and she stops and turns. It's a man who has once been taller than he is now. He's wearing worn black pants, the fly coming undone, a shirt with no buttons, and one of the wool tea-cosy hats; he has no shoes on, the trouser legs look familiar. He stands in front of her and touches her arm, smiling. His jaw is stubbled with white hairs and most of his teeth are missing.

He makes his right hand into a fist, then points to her, still smiling. Rennie smiles back at him. She doesn't understand what he wants. He repeats the gesture, he's deaf and dumb or perhaps drunk. Rennie feels very suddenly as if she's stepped across a line and found herself on Mars.

He runs the fingers of his right hand together, he's getting impatient, he holds out his hand, and now she knows, it's begging. She opens her purse and gropes for the change purse. It's worth a few cents to be rid of him.

But he frowns, this isn't what he wants. He repeats his series of gestures, faster now, and Rennie feels bewildered and threatened. She gets the absurd idea that he wants her passport, he wants to take it away from her. Without it she could never get back. She closes her purse and shakes her head, turning away and starting to walk again. She's being silly; in any case, her passport is in the safe back at the hotel.

Wherever that is. She can feel him behind her, following her. She quickens her pace; the slip-slop of his bare feet speeds up too. Now she's almost running. There are more people on the street, more and more as she runs downhill, and they notice this little procession of two, this race, they even stop to watch, smiling and even laughing, but nobody does anything to help her. Rennie is close to panic, it's too much like the kind of bad dream she wishes she could stop having, she doesn't know why he's following her. What has she done wrong?

There are crowds of people now, it looks like a market, there's a widening that in Mexico would be a square but here is an amorphous shape, the edges packed with stalls, the centre clogged with people and a few trucks. Chickens in crates, fruit stacked into uneasy pyramids or spread out on cloths, plastic pails, cheap aluminium cookware. It's noisy, dusty, suddenly ten degrees hotter; smells engulf her. Music blares from tiny shops crammed with gadgets, the spillover from Japan: cassette players, radios. Rennie dodges among the clumps of people, trying to lose him. But he's right behind her, he's not as decrepit as he looks, and that's his hand on her arm.

"Slow down," says Paul. And it is Paul, in the same shorts but a blue T-shirt, carrying a string bag full of lemons. The man is right behind him, smiling again with his gaping jack-o'-lantern mouth.

"It's okay," says Paul. Rennie's breathing hard, her face is wet and must be red, she probably looks demented and certainly inept. "He just wants you to shake his hand, that's all."

"How do you know?" says Rennie, more angry now than frightened. "He was chasing me!"

"He chases women a lot," says Paul. "Especially the white ones. He's deaf and dumb, he's harmless. He only wants to shake your hand, he thinks it's good luck."

Indeed the man is now holding out his hand, fingers spread.

"Why on earth?" says Rennie. She's a little calmer now but no cooler. "I'm hardly good luck."

"Not for him," says Paul. "For you."

Now Rennie feels both rude and uncharitable: he's only been trying to give her something. Reluctantly she puts her hand into the outstretched hand of the old man. He clamps his fingers around hers and holds on for an instant. Then he lets her go, smiles at her again with his collapsing mouth, and turns away into the crowd.

Rennie feels rescued. "You need to sit down," says Paul. He still has his hand on her arm, and he steers her to a storefront café, a couple of rickety tables covered with oilcloth, and inserts her into a chair next to the wall.

"I'm all right," says Rennie.

"It takes a while for your body to adjust to the heat," says Paul. "You shouldn't run at first."

"Believe me," says Rennie, "I wasn't doing it on purpose."

"Alien reaction paranoia," says Paul. "Because you don't know what's dangerous and what isn't, everything seems dangerous. We used to run into it all the time."

He means in the Far East, he means in the war. Rennie feels he's talking down to her. "Those for scurvy?" she says.

"What?" says Paul.

"On your pirate boats," Rennie says. "The lemons."

Paul smiles and says he'll go inside and order them a drink.

It isn't just a market. Across from the café they've set up a small platform: orange crates stacked two high, with boards across the top. A couple of kids, fifteen or sixteen at the oldest, are draping a bedsheet banner on two poles above it: PRINCE OF PEACE, it says in red. A religious cult of some kind, Rennie decides: Holy Rollers, Born Againers. So the woman in the airport with the Prince of Peace T-shirt wasn't a maniac, just a fanatic. She knows about those: Griswold had its lunatic fringe, women who thought it was a sin to wear lipstick. Then there was her mother, who thought it was a sin not to.

There's a man sitting on the edge of the platform, directing the kids. He's thin, with a riverboat moustache; he slouches forward, dangling his legs. Rennie notices his boots, riding boots, cowboy boots almost, with built-up heels. He's the first man she's seen here wearing boots. Why would anyone choose to? She thinks briefly of his feet, stifled in humid leather.

He sees her watching him. Rennie looks away immediately, but he gets up and comes towards her. He leans his hands on the table and stares down at her. Up close he looks South American.

Now what? thinks Rennie. She assumes he's trying to pick her up, and she's stuck here, wedged in between the table and the wall. She waits for the smile, the invitation, but neither comes, he just frowns at her as if he's trying to read her mind or impress her, so finally she says, "I'm with someone."

"You come in on the plane last night?" he says.

Rennie says yes.

"You the writer?"

Rennie wonders how he knows, but he does, because he doesn't wait for her to answer. "We don't need you here," he says.

Rennie's heard that the Caribbean is becoming hostile to tourists, but this is the most blatant sign she's seen of it. She doesn't know what to say.

"You stay around here, you just mess things up," he says.

Paul is coming back, with two glasses full of something brown. "Government issue," he says, putting them down on the table. "Something the matter?"

"I don't know," says Rennie. "Ask him." But the man is already sauntering away, teetering a little on the uneven ground.

"What did he say to you?" says Paul.

Rennie tells him. "Maybe I'm offending someone's religion," she says.

"It's not religion, it's politics," says Paul, "though around here it's sometimes the same thing."

"Prince of Peace?" says Rennie. "Politics? Come on."

"Well, his name's Prince, really, and the one you just met is Marsdon. He's the campaign manager," says Paul, who doesn't seem to find any of this odd. "They're the local excuse for communists, so they stuck the *Peace* on for good measure."

Rennie tastes the brown drink. "What's in it?" she says.

"Don't ask me," says Paul, "it's all they had." He leans back in his chair, watching not her but the space in front of them. "They're having an election, the first since the British pulled out," he says. "This afternoon they'll make speeches, all three parties, one after the other. Prince, then Dr. Minnow, that's his corner over there. After that the Minister of Justice. He's standing in for Ellis, who never goes outside his house. Some say it's because he's always too drunk; others say he's been dead for twenty years but no one's noticed yet."

"Dr. Minnow?" says Rennie, remembering the man on the

plane. With a name like that there can't be two of them.

"The fish," says Paul, grinning. "They use pictures here, it gets around the illiteracy."

The signs and banners are going up everywhere now. ELLIS IS KING. THE FISH LIVES. Everything looks homemade: it's like college, like student elections.

"Will there be trouble?" says Rennie.

"You mean, will you get hurt?" says Paul. "Yes, there will be trouble. No, you won't get hurt. You're a tourist, you're exempt."

There's a truck making its way through the crowd now, slowly; in the back is a man wearing a white shirt and mirror sunglasses, barking at the crowd through a bullhorn loud-speaker. Rennie can't understand a word he's saying. Two other men flank him, carrying placards with large black crowns on them. ELLIS IS KING. "The Minister of Justice," says Paul.

"What sort of trouble?" says Rennie, wondering if she can get a refund on her excursion ticket if she goes back early.

"A little pushing and shoving," says Paul. "Nothing to get excited about."

But already people are throwing things at the truck; fruit, Rennie thinks, they're picking it up from the stacks on the sidewalk. A crumpled beer can hits the wall above Rennie's head, bounces off.

"They weren't aiming at you," says Paul. "But I'll walk you back to the hotel. Sometimes they get into the broken glass."

He moves the table to let her out, and they push their way through the crowd, against the stream. Rennie wonders if she should ask him about tennis courts and restaurants but decides not to. Her image is fluffy enough already. Then she wonders if she should ask him to have lunch with her at the hotel, but she decides not to do that either. She might be misunderstood.

●

Which is just as well, considering the lunch. Rennie has a grilled cheese sandwich, burned, and a glass of grapefruit juice out of a tin, which seems to be all there is. After the Jello pie she takes out the map of Queenstown and pores over it with vague desperation; she has the unpleasant feeling that she's already seen just about everything there is to see. There's a reef, though, on the other side of the jetty that marks off the harbour; you can go out in a boat and look at it. The picture in the brochure shows a couple of murky fish. It doesn't look too promising, but it might yield a paragraph or two.

The map shows a shortcut to the sea. Rennie envisioned a road, but it's only a rudimentary path; it runs behind the hotel, beside something that looks like a sewage pipe. The ground is damp and slippery. Rennie picks her way down, wishing her sandals had flat soles.

The beach isn't one of the seven jewel-like beaches with clean sparkling iridescent sand advertised in the brochure. It's narrow and gravelly and dotted with lumps of coagulated oil, soft as chewing gum and tar-coloured. The sewage pipe runs into the sea. Rennie steps over it and walks left. She passes a shed and a hauled-up rowboat where three men are cutting the heads off fish, gutting them and tossing them into a red plastic pail. Bladders like used condoms litter the beach. One of the men grins at Rennie and holds up a fish, his finger hooked through the gills. Rennie shakes her head. She might take their picture and write something about the catch fresh from the sea and down-to-earth lifestyles. But then she would have to buy a fish, and she can't carry a dead fish around with her all day.

"What time you meet me tonight?" one of the men says behind her. Rennie ignores this.

In the distance there are two boats with awnings, more or less where the map says they should be. She plods along the beach; when she's well past the fish heads she takes off her sandals and walks on the wet packed sand near the water. To the left she can now see the mountains, rising steeply behind the town, covered with uniform nubbled green.

The boats don't leave until high tide. She buys a ticket from the owner of the nearest and newest-looking one, *The Princess Anne*, and sits on the raspy grass in the shade of a bush. The other boat is called *The Princess Margaret*. There's hardly a lineup: a grey-haired couple with binoculars and the ingenuous, eager-to-be-pleased look of retired Americans from the Midwest, and two girls in their teens, white and speckled. They're both wearing T-shirts with mottoes: TRY A VIRGIN (ISLAND), PROPERTY OF ST. MARTIN'S COUNTY JAIL. There's half an hour to wait. The girls peel off their T-shirts and shorts; they're wearing bikinis underneath. They sit out on the filthy beach, rubbing oil on each other's parboiled backs. Skin cancer, thinks Rennie.

Her own dress comes up to her neck. Although it's sleeveless she's already too warm. She gazes at the deceptively blue sea; even though she knows what kind of garbage runs into it nearby, she longs to wade in it. But she hasn't been swimming since the operation. She hasn't yet found a bathing suit that will do: this is her excuse. Her real fear, irrational but a fear, is that the scar will come undone in the water, split open like a faulty zipper, and she will turn inside out. Then she would see what Daniel saw when he looked into her, while she herself lay on the table unconscious as a slit fish. This is partly why she fell in love with him: he knows something about her she doesn't know, he knows what she's like inside.

●

Rennie takes the three postcards out of her purse, "St. Anthony by an early unknown local artist." She addresses one of them to her mother in Griswold. Her mother still lives in Griswold, even though her grandmother is dead and there's no reason at all why her mother can't move, travel, do something else. But she stays in Griswold, cleaning the red brick house that seems to get bigger and both emptier and more cluttered every time Rennie visits it. Where else would I go? says her mother. It's too late. Besides, my friends are here.

One of Rennie's less pleasant fantasies about the future, on nights when she can't sleep, is that her mother will get some lingering disease and she'll have to go back to Griswold to take care of her, for years and years, for the rest of her life. She'll plead illness, they'll have a competition, the sickest one will win. That's how it's done in Griswold, by the women at any rate. Rennie can remember her mother's church group in the front parlour, drinking tea and eating small cakes covered with chocolate icing and poisonous-looking many-coloured sprinkles, discussing their own and each other's debilities in hushed voices that blended pity, admiration and envy. If you were sick you were exempt: other women brought you pies and came to sit with you, commiserating, gloating. The only thing they liked better was a funeral.

On the card Rennie writes that she's well and is having a nice relaxing time. She hasn't told her mother about Jake leaving, since it was hard enough to get her to accept the fact that he'd moved in. Rennie would have dodged that one if she could, but her mother was fond of phoning her early in the morning, at a time when she thought everyone ought to be up, and the phone was on Jake's side of the bed. It would have been better if Jake weren't in the habit of disguising his voice and saying things like "The White House" and "Fiedlefort's Garage." Rennie finally had to explain to her mother that it was only one male voice she was hearing, not several. Which was only marginally acceptable. After that, they didn't discuss it.

Rennie hasn't told her mother about the operation, either. She stopped telling her mother bad news a long time ago. As a child, she learned to conceal cuts and scrapes, since her mother seemed to regard such things not as accidents but as acts Rennie committed on purpose to complicate her mother's life. What did you do *that* for, she would say, jabbing at the blood with a towel. Next time, watch where you're going. The operation, too, she would see as Rennie's fault. Cancer was a front-parlour subject, but it wasn't in the same class as a broken leg or a heart attack or even a death. It was apart, obscene almost, like a scandal; it was something you brought upon yourself.

Other people think that too, but in different ways. Rennie used to think it herself. *Sexual repression. Couldn't act out anger.* The body, sinister twin, taking its revenge for whatever crimes the mind was supposed to have committed on it. Nothing had prepared her for her own outrage, the feeling that she'd been betrayed by a close friend. She'd given her body swimming twice a week, forbidden it junk food and cigarette smoke, allowed it a normal amount of sexual release. She'd trusted it. Why then had it turned against her?

Daniel talked about the importance of attitude. It's mysterious, he said. We don't know why, but it helps, or it seems to.

What does? she said.

Hope, he said. The mind isn't separate from the body; emotions trigger chemical reactions and vice versa, you know that.

So it's my fault if there's a recurrence? I have cancer of the mind? said Rennie.

It isn't a symbol, it's a disease, said Daniel patiently. We just don't know the cure yet. We have a few clues, that's all. We're looking for the X factor. But we'll get it sooner or later and then people like me will be obsolete. He patted her hand. You'll be fine, he said. You have a life to go back to. Unlike some. You're very lucky.

But she was not fine. She was released from the hospital, she went back to the apartment, she still wasn't fine. She longed to be sick again so that Daniel would have to take care of her.

She constructed a program for herself: schedules and goals. She exercised the muscles of her left arm by lifting it and pressing the forearm against the wall, she squeezed a sponge ball in her left hand twenty times a day. She went to movies with Jake to cheer herself up, funny movies, nothing heavy. She began to type again, a page at a time, reworking her drain-chain jewellery piece, picking up where she'd left off. She learned to brush her hair again and to do up buttons. As she did each of these things, she thought of Daniel watching her and approving. Good, he would say. You can do up buttons now? You can brush your own hair? That's right, go to cheerful movies. You're doing really well.

She went for an examination and to get the stitches out. She wore a red blouse, to show Daniel what a positive attitude she had, and sat up straight and smiled. Daniel told her she was doing really well and she began to cry.

He put his arms around her, which was what she'd wanted him to do. She couldn't believe how boring she was being, how stupid, how predictable. Her nose was running. She sniffed, blotted her eyes on Daniel's pocket, in which, she noted, he kept several cheap ballpoint pens, and pushed him away.

I'm sorry, she said. I didn't mean to do that.

Don't be sorry, he said. You're human.

I don't feel human any more, she said. I feel infested. I have bad dreams, I dream I'm full of white maggots eating away at me from the inside.

He sighed. That's normal, he said. You'll get over it.

Stop telling me I'm fucking *normal*, she said.

Daniel checked his list of appointments, looked at his watch, and took her down for a swift coffee in the shopping arcade below his office, where he delivered an earnest lecture. This was the second part of her life. It would be different from the first part, she would not longer be able to take things for granted, but perhaps this was a plus because she would see her life as a gift and appreciate it more. It was almost like being given a second life. She must stop thinking of her life as over, because it was far from over.

When I was a student I used to think I would be able to save people, he said. I don't think that any more. I didn't even think I can cure them; in this field you can't afford to think that. But in a lot of cases we can give them time. A remission can last for years, for a normal lifespan even. He leaned forward slightly. Think of your life as a clean page. You can write whatever you like on it.

Rennie sat across the table from him, white formica with gold threads in it, thinking what a lot of facile crap he was talking and admiring his eyes, which were an elusive shade between blue and green. Where does he get this stuff, she thought, *The Reader's Digest*?

How many times have you used that one? she said. Are you just saying that because I'm a journalist? I mean, if I were a dentist, would you say, Your life is like an empty tooth, you can fill it with whatever you like?

Rennie knew you weren't supposed to say things like this to men you were in love with, or to men in general, or to anyone at all for that matter; making fun was rude, especially when the other person was being serious. But she couldn't resist. He would have had a right to be angry, but instead he was startled. He looked at her for a moment almost slyly; then he began to laugh. He was blushing, and Rennie was entranced: the men she knew didn't blush.

I guess you think that's pretty corny, he said.

Corny. My God, thought Rennie. I'm caught in a time warp, it's nineteen fifty-five again. He's from another planet.

I'm sorry, she said. I get pretty surly at times. It's just that, what am I supposed to do with it? All this time I've got. Sit around waiting till it gets me? You know it's going to, sooner or later.

He gazed at her sadly, disappointed again, as if she were talking like a spoiled child. Do what you want to, he said. What you really want to.

What would you do? She said. She fought the impulse to interview him. "When Doctors Get Sick."

He looked down at his hands. What I'm doing now, I guess, he said. That's about all I know anything about. But you have an interesting life.

This was the first clue Rennie had that Daniel thought she was interesting.

Rennie looks at the other two postcards. She addresses one to Jake, it would be a courtesy to let him know where she is, but she doesn't write anything on it because she can't think of anything she wants to say to him. The third one she leaves empty. Empty is not the same as clean. She bought the third one for Daniel but she decides not to send it. She'll send it later, when she can say, *I'm fine*. That's what he would like to hear: that she's fine, that everything is fine, that he's done no damage.

●

Rennie feels a darker shadow fall over her. "Hi there," says a flat nasal voice, mildly familiar. It's the woman who passed her in the hotel last night. She now sits down beside Rennie uninvited and takes a pack of cigarettes out of her bag. Rennie puts away her postcards.

"You smoke?" says the woman. The fingers holding the cigarette are bitten to the quick, stub-tipped, slightly grubby, the raw skin around the nails as if mice have been at them, and this both surprises Rennie and repels her slightly. She wouldn't want to touch this gnawed hand, or have it touch her. She doesn't like the sight of ravage, damage, the edge between inside and outside blurred like that.

"No, thanks," says Rennie.

"My name's Lora," says the woman, "with an *o*, not the other way. Lora Lucas. *L*'s run in our family, my mother's name was Leona." Now that she's talking, the illusion shatters: "Hi there" is about the only thing she's learned to fake, the rest is natural. She's not as young as she looked in the dim light of the hotel. Her hair is down today, flower-child length, dry as hay. She's wearing an above-the-knee oblong of orange knotted across her large breasts.

Her eyes are scanning, all the time, back and forth, taking everything in. "You just come in, eh?" she says, and Rennie thinks, *Canadian*.

"Yes," says Rennie.

"You got to watch it around here," says Lora. "People see you don't know what you're doing, they rip you off. How much he soak you from the airport last night?"

Rennie tells her and she laughs. "You see?" she says.

Rennie immediately resents her, she resents the intrusion. She wishes she had a book; then she could pretend to read.

"You should watch your stuff, that camera and all," says Lora. "There's been some break-ins around here. A girl I know, she woke up in the middle of the night and there was this black guy in a bathing suit holding a knife to her throat. Nothing sexual, he just wanted her money. Said he'd kill her if she told anyone. She was afraid to go to the police."

"Why?" Rennie says, and Lora grins at her.

"She figures he *was* the police," she says.

In response to some signal Rennie hasn't caught, she stands up and brushes the sand from her orange tie dye. "Boat time," she says. "If that's what you're here for."

It seems they're expected to wade out to the boat. The old couple with the matching binoculars go first. They're both wearing wide-legged khaki shorts, which they roll up even farther, exposing stringy whitish legs which are surprisingly muscular. Even so, the drooping bottoms of their shorts are wet through by the time they reach the boat's ladder. The two speckled pink girls make it with a lot of shrieking. Lora unties her tie dye, under which she's wearing a black bikini half a size too small, and drapes it around her neck. She holds the purple cloth bag she's carrying at shoulder height and surges into the water; surf breaks around her thighs, which bulge out of the bikini like caricatures of thighs, like the thighs on humorous cocktail napkins.

Rennie considers her options. She can either hitch up her dress and tuck it into her underpants, with everyone watching her, or get it wet and smell like seaweed for the rest of the day. She compromises, hiking her skirt halfway up and draping it through the sash tie. It gets wet anyway. The man who appears to own the boat smiles widely as the swell hits her. He reaches out a long ropy arm, a hand like a clamp, to help her up. At the last moment, when the motor is already running, five or six children come screaming and laughing out through the waves and swarm onto the boat, clambering up onto the awning, which Rennie now sees is wooden rather than cloth.

"Mind yourself, you fall off," the owner yells at them.

Rennie sits on the wooden bench, dripping, while the boat goes up and down and the exhaust blows into her face. Lora has gone up on top where the kids are, probably to work on her tan. The two girls are flirting with the man running the boat. The old couple are looking at sea birds through their binoculars, murmuring to each other in what sounds like a secret language. "Booby," the old woman says. "Frigate," the man replies.

In front of Rennie is a raised ledge bordering an oblong piece of glass almost the length of the boat. Rennie leans forward and rests her arm on it. Nothing but greyish foam is visible through the glass. She's doing this, she reminds herself, so she can write about how much fun it is. *At first you may think you could get the same effect for a lot less money by putting a little Tide in your Jacuzzi. But wait.*

Rennie waits, and the boat stops. They're quite far out. Twenty yards from them, surf crashes over an invisible wall, each wave lifting the boat. In the furrows between the waves they sink down until they're only a foot from the reef. It's an illusion, Rennie thinks. She prefers to believe that people who run things know what they're doing, and these people surely would not do anything so dangerous. She doesn't like the idea of a prong of coral suddenly bursting through the glass.

Rennie looks, which is her function. The water is clouded with fine sand. At the edges of the glass oblong, dark shapes flit and are hidden. Below her, so encrusted in purplish coral that its shape is almost obscure, is a soft-drink bottle. A tiger-striped fish swims near it.

"It's not so great today, it's been too windy, and this one's not such a great one anyway," Lora says to her. She's come down from the roof and is kneeling beside Rennie. "The reef's getting all messed up by the oil and junk from the harbour. What you need is a snorkel and stuff, over at Ste. Agathe. That's where I live, you'd like it a lot better than here."

Rennie doesn't say anything; she doesn't seem expected to. Also she doesn't want to start a conversation. Conversations lead to acquaintances, and acquaintances are too easy to make on these trips. People mistake them for friendships. She smiles and turns back to the glass oblong.

"You write for the magazines, eh?" the woman says.

"How did you know that?" Rennie asks, a little annoyed. This is the third time today.

"Everyone knows everything around here," the woman says. "Word of mouth, the grapevine you might say. Everyone knows what's happening." She pauses. She looks at Rennie, scanning her face as if trying to see through the blue lenses of her sunglasses. "I could tell you stuff to write about," she says darkly. "The story of my life, you could put it in a book all right. Except no one would believe it, you know?"

Rennie is instantly bored. She can't remember how many people have said this to her, at parties, on airplanes, as soon as they've found out what she does. Why do they think their own lives are of general concern? Why do they think that being in a magazine will make them more valid than they are? Why do they want to be *seen*?

Rennie switches off the sound and concentrates only on the picture. Lora could definitely be improved. She would benefit greatly from a good cut and shape, for instance, and she should grow her eyebrows in, just a little. Plucking them fine like that broadens her face. Rennie arranges her into a Makeover piece, before and after, with a series of shots in between showing the process, Lora being tweezed and creamed and coloured in and fitted with a Norma Klein sweater. After that you could take her to lunch at Winston's and all you'd have to teach her would be how to keep her mouth shut.

●

They're sitting under a metal umbrella at one of the round white tables on the patio at the Driftwood, Lora with the sun on her back, Rennie in the shade. The other tables are thinly scattered with white people in various phases of hot pink, and one couple who seems to be Indian. The waiters are black or brown; the architecture is roadside modern, the balconies have plastic panels, green and blue. At the edge of the patio there's a tree covered with red flowers, huge lobed blossoms like gigantic sweet peas; a dozen hummingbirds swarm around them. Below, on the other side of the curving stone wall, the surf crashes against the rocks just as it is supposed to, and a fresh wind blows off the Atlantic. To the right is a wide beach devoid of fish heads. There's nobody on it.

Lora orders another piña colada. Rennie is only halfway through hers, but she orders another one anyway.

"Who's paying for this?" Lora asks, too innocently.

"I will," says Rennie, who has always known she would.

"You can put it on your whatchamacallit," Lora says. "Don't they pay for everything, those magazines?"

"Not always," says Rennie, "but I can write it off as an expense. We can pretend I was interviewing you."

"Write it off," says Lora. "Jesus." Rennie can't tell whether she's impressed or disgusted.

"This is where people like you stay, most of the time," says Lora.

Rennie dislikes having these kinds of assumptions made about her, she dislikes being lumped in with a fictitious group labelled *people like you*. She can't stand the self-righteousness of people like Lora, who think that because they've had deprived childhoods or not as much money as everybody else they are in some way superior. She feels like using one of her never-fail ploys. She'll lean across the table, take off her sunglasses, gaze into Lora's round blue-china eyes, eyes that manage to look at the same time aggrieved and secretly delighted, and say, "Why are you being so aggressive?" But she has a feeling this wouldn't work on Lora.

She thinks about unbuttoning her dress and displaying her scar. If they're having a poor-me contest, that should be good for a few points; but she doesn't want to turn into one of those people who use their physical disabilities for social blackmail.

She knows she shouldn't have allowed herself to be picked up on the reef boat, she shouldn't have expressed interest in seeing the other hotels, she should have insisted on a taxi instead of listening to Lora, who said she knew people and why get ripped off when you could get a ride for free? "Free rides, that's my motto," she said. Rennie's mother used to say there was no such thing as a free ride.

The free ride turned out to be a battered pickup truck with two yellow eyes painted on the hood. It was delivering toilet paper, and they had to sit on the boxes in the back, perched up there like float queens; groups of people waved and yelled at them as they went past. Outside the town the road got steadily worse, dwindling finally into a two-wheel track of cracked and disintegrating concrete. The driver went as fast as possible, and every time they hit a gap in the concrete Rennie could feel the top of her spine being rammed up into her skull.

She doesn't want to face the ride back, but she doesn't want to stay here either. If she isn't careful she'll be trapped into having dinner. Lora, she's decided, is one of those women you meet in bars in foreign countries, who seem not to have chosen anything but merely ended up wherever they happen to be, and it's too much effort for them to go home. Rennie can't imagine why Lora has been so insistent about coming with her. They have nothing in common. Lora says she has nothing else to do at the moment so she might as well show Rennie around, but Rennie doesn't believe this. She resolves to finish her drink and then go. If she's lucky it will rain: promising clouds are already piling up.

Now Lora opens her purple bag and rustles through it, and suddenly everything falls into place. What she takes out is a poly bag of grass, about an ounce, Rennie guesses. She wants Rennie to buy it. The price, by Toronto standards, is ridiculously low.

"The best," she says. "Colombian, it just came in."

Rennie of course refuses. She's heard about dope laws in foreign countries, she knows about being set up, she has no intention of spending any time at all growing fungus in the local jail while the local bureaucrats try, unsuccessfully, to put the squeeze on her mother. Her mother is a firm believer in taking the consequences for your actions. And who else would get her out? Who would even try?

Lora shrugs. "It's cool," she says. "No harm in asking."

Rennie looks around to see what has become of Lora's drink, and feels herself turn cold.

"My God," she says.

There are two policemen in the bar, they're going from table to table, it looks as if they're asking questions. But Lora stares calmly over at them, she doesn't even put the dope away, she just moves her cloth bag so it's covered. "Don't look so weird," she says to Rennie. "It's cool. I wouldn't say it was cool if it wasn't."

And it turns out after all that they're just selling tickets to the Police Benefit Dance. Rennie thinks she recognizes them from the airport, but she's not sure. One sells, the other stands behind him, dangling his swagger stick and checking out the scene. She produces her own ticket from her purse. "I already have one," she says, a little too smugly, because the one selling grins at her and says, "You need two, man. One for your boyfriend. Some things you can't do by yourself."

The second one laughs, a high giggle.

"That's a real good idea," says Lora, smiling a little tightly, her Holiday Inn smile; so Rennie pays.

"We see you there," says the first policeman, and they saunter off.

"If there's one thing I hate it's cops," says Lora, when they're hardly out of earshot. "They're all in the business if you ask me, one way or another, I've got nothing against that but they take advantage. It's unfair competition. You ever been stopped by a cop? For speeding or anything? Back home I mean, around here they don't bother that much about speeding."

"No," says Rennie.

"They look at your driver's licence. Then they use your first name. Not Miss or Mrs. or anything, your first name, and you've got no way of knowing any of their names at all. You ever have that happen to you?"

In fact Rennie hasn't. She's having trouble paying attention, there's too much rum in the drinks. Lora, however, has just signalled for another one, it's not bothering her.

"That's where it begins," says Lora. "Where they can use your first name and you can't use theirs. Then they think they've got you, they can look down on you, like. Sometimes they give you a choice, fork out or put out."

"Sorry?" says Rennie.

"You know, pay the fine or go down on them. They always know where the vacant lots are, eh?"

Lora looks at her slyly and Rennie knows she's supposed to be shocked. "Really," she says, as if she's been through it herself, dozens of times.

The Women's Movement would have loved Lora, back in the old days, back in the early seventies when they were still doing pieces about the liberating effects of masturbation. They'd have given her ten out of ten for openness, a word that always made Rennie think of a can of worms with the top off. Nevertheless, Rennie did several pieces on the movement back then, until its media potential burned out. Then she did a piece called "Burned Out": interviews with eight women who'd explained why they'd gone into weaving placemats and painting miniature landscapes on bottles, instead. It was the infighting, they said. The bitching. The trashing. Other women were just so difficult to work with, you never knew where you stood with them. And it all went on behind your back. At least with men it was out on the table, they said; and Rennie busily wrote it all down.

Great stuff, said the editor. It's about time someone had the courage to speak out.

Lora smiles but she's not fooled; she can tell this is one of the things Rennie doesn't know. But she's generous, she's willing to share. Ten out of ten for sharing.

"Listen," she says, "at least you have the choice. You can always say you're worth more than a speeding ticket. I don't know which is worse though, no choice at all or just a lot of bad ones. At least when you don't have a choice you don't have to think, you know? The worst times in my life I had choices all right. Shit or shit."

Rennie doesn't want to hear about the worst times in Lora's life, so she doesn't say anything.

"Anyway, why dwell on it?" says Lora. "That's what my

mother used to say. There's enough bad things in the world, there's no shortage, so why dwell on it, there's better things to talk about."

Rennie wonders what these may be, since Lora can't seem to think of any. She slurps at the bottom of her glass with the two plastic straws. "You like maraschino cherries?" she says. "I can't stand them."

Rennie hesitates. She does like maraschino cherries, but she isn't sure she wants to eat the one Lora is now poking around for at the bottom of the glass with her bitten fingers. However, she's about to be rescued, because Paul has just stepped out on to the patio and is standing there scanning the tables as though he's looking for someone.

Rennie knows it's her. She waves, and he strolls over to their table.

"What have you been up to?" he says, smiling at her.

"Research," says Rennie, smiling back.

"You're late," Lora says to him. "I've been here for hours."

"I'll get myself a drink," he says, and walks over to the bar.

"Just a sec," says Lora. "Would you mind keeping an eye on my bag?" She stands up, pushes back her hair, straightens up so her breasts stick out more, and walks over to join Paul. They stand there talking, for a lot longer than Rennie wants them to.

The third piña colada comes, the one for Lora, and Rennie drinks some of it, for something to do.

●

Lora comes back from the bar and sits down. Her drink is there but she doesn't touch it. Something has happened, her face is no longer a dollface. Rennie notices the skin under her eyes, too much sun, in a few years she'll shrivel up like an apple. She looks at Rennie, dolefully as a spaniel.

"What's wrong?" says Rennie, knowing as she says it that she shouldn't have asked. To ask is to get involved.

"Look," says Lora, "can you do me a big favour?"

"What?" says Rennie, on guard.

"Elva's sick," she says, "that's Prince's grandmother. Over on Ste. Agathe."

"Prince?" says Rennie. There can't be two of them.

"The guy I live with," Lora says.

"The one in the election?" says Rennie, who can't quite put it together.

"That's why he can't go over to Ste. Agathe," says Lora, "he's making a speech today, so I have to, she sort of lives with us. She's eighty-two, it's her heart, and there's no doctors over there and nobody to, you know. So I have to get over there right away." Is it possible she's almost crying?

"What can I do?" says Rennie. In Griswold it would be cupcakes or a pumpkin pie. This is familiar ground. She's friendlier towards Lora now that she knows Lora's living with someone. Who is not Paul.

"There's this box coming into the airport tomorrow," says Lora, "you think you can pick it up for me?"

Rennie is immediately suspicious. "What's in it?" she says.

Lora looks at her and manages a grin. "Not what you think," she says. "There's one thing around here you don't have to get mailed in from New York, that's for sure. It's her heart medicine. She's got this daughter there sends it to her all the time. You can't get stuff like that here. She ran out of it, that's why she got sick."

Rennie does not want the death of an eighty-two-year-old grandmother on her hands. What can she say but yes? You're too distrustful, Jake used to tell her. Try the benefit of the doubt for once in your life.

Paul walks over, he's taking his time, he never seems to move very fast. He puts his half-empty drink on the table and sits down. He smiles, but Lora doesn't even look at him.

"What you need to do," Lora says, "you need to go there tomorrow morning around eight, the window that says Customs. Here, you need this thing here. It has to be around eight." She rummages in her purple bag, she can't seem to find it. Finally she takes out a creased and folded piece of paper. "Right," she says. "Just say she sent you and give them this. You ask for this fellow called Harold, he should be there; if he's not you have to wait."

Rennie takes the paper; it's a simple customs notice. There's nothing to pay, no complications. "Why can't I just hand it in at the window?" she says. "Anyone should be able to deal with this."

Lora gives her a patient but exasperated look. "You don't know how they do things around here," she says. "He's the one I gave the bribe to. If you don't do that, they just open it up and keep half the stuff. Or they might keep all of it and never tell you it got here, you know? Sell it on the black market."

"Really?" says Rennie.

"Every place has a different system," says Lora. "But they've all got one. You just need to figure out how it works." She's more relaxed now, she siphons up the rest of her piña colada and stands, scraping back the metal chair. "I got to go to the can," she says, and disappears into the main building.

Rennie and Paul are left sitting together. "Can I get you another?" Paul says.

"No thanks," says Rennie. She's on the edge of being quite drunk. "How do I get back from here?" She realizes this sounds like a request. "I'll call a taxi," she says.

"Taxis don't like to come out here," Paul says. "The roads are too bad, they don't like to wreck their springs. Anyway, you'd have to wait for hours. I'll give you a lift, I've got a jeep out front."

"Only if you're going back anyway," says Rennie.

He stands up, he's ready to leave right now. "What about Lora?" says Rennie. She doesn't want to ride back with Lora, but it would be rude to leave her stranded.

"She'll get back on her own all right," Paul says. "She knows a lot of people."

On the way out Rennie sees Lora, who isn't in the can after all but is standing near the kitchen door, talking with one of the waiters. Rennie goes over to say goodbye.

"Have a nice time," Lora says, with her Holiday Inn smile. She presses something into Rennie's hand; it feels like a wad of Kleenex. "It's a gift," she says. "You're doing me a favour."

"Is Lora a friend of yours?" Rennie asks when they're outside, walking across the Driftwood's thick lawn.

"How do you mean?" says Paul.

Rennie founders. She doesn't want to reveal jealousy or even interest, though she suddenly realizes that she feels both. "I mean, do you know her very well?"

"Well enough," says Paul. "She's been around for a while."

"She seems to be living with some man, over on Ste. Agathe," Rennie says.

"Prince?" Paul says. "Not exactly. Off and on, the way they do. He's into politics, she's not."

"She seems to be into just about everything else," says Rennie.

Paul doesn't say anything, he's staying completely neutral. Rennie's real question hasn't been answered and she can see it won't be.

They reach the driveway and find the jeep, which is small and battered, with open sides and a canvas top. "Is it yours?" Rennie says.

"Friend of mine's," says Paul. He doesn't open the door for her and it takes her a while to get it open for herself. She's definitely had too much to drink. Paul takes out a pair of mirror sunglasses and puts them on. Then he turns the key. The jeep scoots backwards into the ditch, which seems to be the only way to turn around, then accelerates forward, wheels spinning in the mud. Rennie clamps her right hand to the metal frame at the top, her left to the seat, which is also metal. There are no safety belts.

They drive through the forest that surrounds the Driftwood, huge hothouse trees draped with creepers, giant prehistoric ferns, obese plants with rubbery ear-shaped leaves and fruit like warts, like glands. Some of the trees have toppled over, tearing up swaths of earth, their thick snarled roots in the air now.

"Allan," Paul yells over the noise of the jeep.

"What?" says Rennie.

"The hurricane."

Now they're in a coconut plantation. It seems to be abandoned, some of the trees are dead, the coconuts are everywhere, on the road even, the road is worse here, they're hitting every pothole. Rennie's hands are cold, she's sweating, she no longer feels drunk but she thinks she's going to be sick.

"Could you stop?" she shouts.

"What?" says Paul.

"Stop!" she says. "Please stop!"

He looks over at her, then pulls the jeep off to the side of the road. Rennie puts her head down on her knees she'll be all right if she can just stay like this for a minute. It's a drag, stopping like this, she feels silly, but it's better than vomiting on him. "Throwing Up In the Sun," she thinks briefly. Tippy would say everything's raw material, you just have to know how to work it in.

Paul touches her back. "Any better?" he says. "I guess I was driving too fast for you."

With her head down Rennie listens, she can hear birds, thin shrill voices like fingernails, raucous croaks, insects, her heart going too fast. After a while, she doesn't know how long, she lifts her head. Paul is looking at her, his face is right there, she can see two little faces, white and tiny, reflected back at her from his sunglasses. Without his eyes his face is expressionless, he's a faceless stranger. She's aware of his arm lying across the back of the seat.

"Could you take off your sunglasses, please?" she says.

"Why?" he says, but he does.

Rennie turns her head away from him. It's late, the sun is slanting down through the long spokes of the palm trees, the coconuts lie rotting in their husks; here and there something, an animal, has made large burrows in the ground.

"What lives in the holes?" says Rennie.

"Landcrabs," Paul says. "Big white buggers. They only come out at night, you hunt them with a flashlight and a big stick. You shine the light in their eyes, that stops them and then you pin them down with the stick."

"Can you eat them?" Rennie says. She's still not connecting very well: the outlines are too clear, the sounds too sharp.

"Sure, if you want to," Paul says. "That's why you hunt them."

He turns her around to face him, he's smiling, he kisses her, more exploration than passion. After a minute Rennie puts her hand on the back of his neck; the hair is soft, she can feel the muscles under it, the ropes, the knots. His hand moves towards her breast, she takes hold of it, slides her fingers between his own. He looks at her and nods a little. "Right," he says. "Let's go back." The rest of the way he drives slowly; it's dark by the time they reach the town.

Rennie wants everything to be easy, why not? Once it would have been, there would have been nothing to it. She likes him, well enough but not too well, she knows nothing about him, she doesn't need to know anything, he knows nothing about her, it's perfect. She walks down the wooden corridor, past the chilly eyes of the Englishwoman, he's just behind her, this is something she wants to do, again, finally, she wants it so much her hands are shaking.

But at the door of her room she turns, without unlocking the door, she can't do it. She can't take that risk.

"I take it I'm coming in?" he says.

She says no, but there's nothing more she can say.

He shrugs. "Up to you," he says. She has no idea what he

thinks. He kisses her on the cheek, a peck, and walks away down the green corridor.

●

Rennie goes into her room, locks the door, and sits down on the edge of the bed. After a while she opens her purse. From the zipper compartment at the back she takes out the Kleenex package Lora handed her and unwraps it. Inside, there's what she knew there would be, five joints, tightly and expertly rolled. She's grateful.

She picks one and lights it with a wooden Swedish match. She smokes a little of it, just enough to relax, puts it out and slides the remaining half and the other four joints between the folds of the green blanket in the middle drawer of the bureau. She lies down on the bed again, hearing the blood running through her body, which is still alive. She thinks of the cells, whispering, dividing in darkness, replacing each other one at a time; and of the other cells, the evil ones which may or may not be there, working away in her with furious energy, like yeast. They would show up hot orange under one kind of light, hot blue under another, like the negative print of the sun when you close your eyes. Beautiful colours.

They use it now in hospitals for terminal cases, it's the one thing that can stop the nausea. She pictures all those Baptists and Presbyterians, no longer sitting in their upright pews but laid out in rows in clean white crank-up beds, stoned to the gills. Of course they call it something else, some respectable Latin name. She wonders how much pain she could take before she would give herself up, give herself over again to the probers, the labellers and cutters. *Doctored*, they say of drinks that have been tampered with, of cats that have been castrated.

You just feel this way about me because I'm your doctor, Daniel said. I'm a fantasy for you. It's normal.

I don't mean to be rude, said Rennie, but if I was going to have a fantasy why would I pick you?

It would be nice to have someone on the bed with her. Almost anyone, as long as he would keep still. Sometimes she wanted just to be still.

You're using me for a teddy bear, Jake said. Why don't you go back to sucking your thumb?

You wouldn't like the substitution, she said. Is there something wrong with quiet companionship?

No, he said, but not every night.

Sometimes I think you don't like me very much, she said.

Like? he said. Is that all you want to be? Liked? Wouldn't you rather be passionately and voraciously desired?

Yes, she said, but not every night.

That was before. After, he said, You're cutting yourself off.

That's a bad pun, she said.

Never give a sucker an even break, he said. What can I do if you won't let me touch you? You don't even want to talk about it.

What aspect of it would you like to discuss? she said. Instances of recurrence? My chances of survival? You want statistics?

Stop talking like a sick joke, he said.

It may be a sick joke but it's what I'm stuck with, she said. That's why I don't want to discuss it. I *know* it's a sick joke. So I'd rather not, if you don't mind.

How you feel, he said. Try that.

How I feel? Great. I feel great. I feel like the body beautiful. How do you want me to feel?

Come on, he said. So it's the end of the world?

Not yet, she said. Not for you.

You're relentless, Jake said.

101

Why? she said. Because I don't feel like it in the same way any more? Because I don't believe you do either?

She used to think sex wasn't an issue, it wasn't crucial, it was a pleasant form of exercise, better than jogging, a pleasant form of communication, like gossip. People who got too intense about sex were a little *outré*. It was like wearing plastic spikes with rhinestones and meaning it, it was like taking mink coats seriously. What mattered was the relationship. A good relationship: that was what she and Jake were supposed to have. People commented on it at parties, as if they were admiring a newly renovated house.

That was what it had been at first: no mess, no *in love*. By the time she met Jake she'd decided she didn't much like being in love. Being in love was like running barefoot along a street covered with broken bottles. It was foolhardly, and if you got through it without damage it was only by sheer luck. It was like taking off your clothes at lunchtime in a bank. It let people think they knew something about you that you didn't know about them, it gave them power over you. It made you visible, soft, penetrable; it made you ludicrous.

There was no question about love with Jake, at first. Not that he wasn't attractive, not that he wasn't possible. He wasn't deformed or a fool and he was good at what he did, he was even good enough to have started his own small company by the time he was thirty. This was how she'd met him: she'd been doing a piece for *Visor* on men who had started their own small companies by the time they were thirty. "The Young and The Solvent," it was called. They'd used Jake for the full-page picture facing the title, and when she thought about him that was the first image she always saw: Jake, "saturnine" she'd called him in the piece, with his dark skin and white teeth and narrow muzzle, grinning like a fox, perched with jaunty irony at his drawing board, wearing a navy blue three-piece suit to prove you didn't didn't have to stroke his ego, he did that for himself.

He decided she should wear nothing but white linen jumpsuits, with shoulder pads. The Rosie the Riveter look, he said.

They make my ass look big, she said.

That's the point, he said. Small asses have been done.

Rennie drew the line at *nothing but* – Let's not be absolutist, she said – but she got one, to please him, though she refused to wear it out on the street. In the livingroom he hung blowups of Cartier-Bresson photographs, three Mexican prostitutes looking out of wooden cubicles, their eyebrows plucked thin and drawn into exaggerated bows, their mouths clown-mouths, an old man sitting in a field of deserted chairs.

That was the daytime. When he had that arranged, he started on the night. In the bedroom he hung a Heather Cooper poster, a brown-skinned woman wound up in a piece of material that held her arms to her sides but left her breasts and thighs and buttocks exposed. She had no expression on her face, she was just standing there, if anything a little bored. The picture was called *Enigma*. The other picture on the bedroom was a stylized print of a woman lying on a 1940s puffy sofa, like the one in their own livingroom. She was feet-first, and her head, up at the other end of the sofa, was tiny, featureless, and rounded like a doorknob. In the foreground there was a bull.

These pictures made Rennie slightly nervous, especially when she was lying on their bed with no clothes on. But that was probably just her background.

Put your arms over your head, Jake said, it lifts the breasts. Move your legs apart, just a little, raise your left knee. You look fantastic.

A secure woman is not threatened by her partner's fantasies, Rennie told herself. As long as there is trust. She'd even written that, or something like it, in a piece on the comeback of satin lingerie and fancy garter belts. And she was not threatened, not for some time.

105

You're so closed, Jake said once. I like that. I want to be the one you open up for.

But she could never remember afterwards what he had actually said. Perhaps he'd said, I want to be the one who opens you up.

M y father came home every Christmas, says Rennie. He always spoke of it as coming home, though it became obvious at last, even to me, that his home was elsewhere. He'd gone to Toronto soon after I was born, he'd been in the war and got university free as a veteran. He studied chemical engineering. He stayed there, everyone said, because the jobs were there. We couldn't go because my grandfather got sick and my grandmother needed the help, that's what they said, and after my grandfather died my grandmother could not be left alone. People in Griswold had a great fear of being left alone. It was supposed to be bad for you, it made you go funny, it drove you bats. Then you had to be put in the loony bin.

So my father would turn up every Christmas. He would stay in one of the guest bedrooms, we had a lot of them, bedrooms that had once been for children and now stood empty, dustless and smelling of lavender and dead air. These visits of his, I was told later, were for my sake. My father and I would be bundled up and sent for walks on the icy streets; both of us would be told not to fall down. He would ask me how I was doing at school and tell me that soon I would be able to come and visit him. Neither of us believed this. On the main street people's heads would turn, not too abruptly, as we went past, and I would know that we were being looked at and discussed.

When I was in Grade Six, two girls, the kind from loose families, spread the story that my father was living with another woman in Toronto, and that was the real reason my mother didn't go to join him. I didn't believe this, but I didn't ask my mother about it either, so I probably did believe it after all. Just as well, because it was true, and when my mother finally told me I wasn't surprised. She waited until my thirteenth birthday, two weeks after my first period. She must have felt I was ready for pain.

I think she wanted sympathy, she felt that at last I would understand what a hard life she had led and what sacrifices she had been forced to make. She hoped I would blame my father, see him in his true light. But I was unable to feel what I was supposed to; instead I blamed her. I was angry with him, not for leaving – I could see why he would have wanted to do that – but for leaving me behind.

By that time he'd stopped coming back for Christmas, though he still sent cards, to me but not to her, and I didn't see him again until I moved to Toronto to go to university. For years he'd been married to someone I thought of only as *her*, because that's what my mother called her. I'd forgotten what he looked like.

I visited them at their apartment. I had never been in an apartment before. That was the first time I'd ever seen a house plant that wasn't an African violet or a poinsettia. They had a lot of plants, hanging all over the southern windows, things I didn't know the names for. There was space between the furniture in their apartment, a lot more space than I was used to. The first thing he said to me was *You look like your mother*. And that was the end of him.

●

When I was growing up, says Lora, we lived in cellars. We lived in the cellars of apartment buildings; they were always dark, even in summer, and they smelled like cat piss, partly because of Bob's cats, he never emptied the litter box even though they were his cats, and partly because those kinds of places always smelled like cat piss anyway. Bob got the apartments for next to nothing, they were the caretaker's apartments, he was supposed to take out the garbage and mop the floors and fix people's toilets, but he was never much good at that, or maybe he didn't want to, which is why we were always moving.

His war buddy Pat used to say that wasn't how Bob really made his money anyway. He said Bob made his money by catching things that fell off the backs of lorries. I didn't figure out for a while that *lorry* was the English word for truck, Pat was from England, and then I didn't believe it, because I knew Bob didn't chase after trucks waiting for stuff to fall off them. He was home most of the time, sitting at the kitchen table in his old grey cardigan, and besides he couldn't run because of his limp. This was lucky for me: if I could keep him from grabbing me I could always outrun him, but he was fast with the hands, he'd pretend he was looking the other way and then snatch, and when I was small he could keep hold of me with one hand while he got his belt off with the other. I guess that's partly what made me so quick on my feet.

He said he got the limp in the war and it was typical of the government that they wouldn't give him a pension. He was against the government, whoever was in, he said it didn't matter a tinker's piss, but don't get the wrong idea, he was death on communism too. He couldn't stand the idea of welfare, that was communism as far as he was concerned. Bob's war buddy Pat used to talk about the working class, he used to say that's what they were, the both of them, but that was always a big joke to me. Working class my ass. Bob worked as little as he could. His whole thing was how you could avoid working, he thought anyone with a steady job was the world's number-one dummy. He was dead against the unions too, he had no sympathy for them at all, he said

111

they just made things more expensive for everybody else. When there were strikes on the TV he would cheer on the police, which was something, because the rest of the time he was dead against them too.

Anyway, it took me a long time to figure out why we would suddenly have five television sets, then none, then eight radios, then only one. Sometimes it was toasters, sometimes it was record players, you never knew. Things appeared and disappeared around our place like magic. I got the belt for bragging at school that we had five television sets, I brought one of the kids over to see, which made Bob mad as hell. This'll teach you to keep your fuckin' lip zipped, he said.

A lot of things made him mad as hell. It was like he spent the whole day sitting at that table, smoking Black Cat cigarettes the way he did and waiting for something to come along and make him mad, and my mother spent the whole day trying to guess what it would be so she could stop it from happening.

Go *around* him, she told me. Why do you have to walk right into him all the time? Pretend he's a closed door. You wouldn't walk right into a door if you could help it, would you? I thought when she said stuff like this she was taking his side, but now I see she was just trying to keep me from getting beat up too much.

I hated him more than anything. I used to lie awake at nights thinking up bad things that could happen to him, like falling down a sewer or getting eaten by rats. There were rats in our apartments, too, or anyway mice, and Bob wouldn't let my mother put out poison because the mice might eat it and then the cats might eat the mice, though his cats never ate any mice that I ever saw. When he wasn't there, which wasn't all that often, I used to step on the cats' tails and chase them around with the broom. I couldn't do anything to him but I sure could make life miserable for his bloody cats. I still can't stand to have a cat near me.

It was mean on the cats, but I think I did stuff like that so I wouldn't have to be scared of him. Remember that story in the papers, six, seven years ago? It was about this woman with a little boy, who married this man, and after a while the two of them killed the little boy, out in the woods. They said they were taking him on a picnic. There was a picture of the little boy that broke my heart. The man just didn't want him around, I guess, and the mother went along with it. I was grown up by the time I read that, I was almost thirty, but it put me in a cold sweat and I dreamed about it off and on for weeks. It was like something that almost happened to me and I didn't even know it at the time, like you're sleepwalking and you wake up and you're standing on the edge of this cliff. I was always more scared of Bob when he was trying to be nice than when he was mad. It's like knowing there's someone in the closet waiting for you but not being able to see in.

My mother married Bob after my father died, that would be when I was around four. I don't know why she married him. My mother wasn't religious or anything, we didn't go to church, but she had this belief that things were ordered, *meant to be* she would say. When I asked her why she married Bob she would say it was meant to be. I don't know who by, somebody with a pretty poor sense of humour if you ask me. She never did figure out that some things are just accidents. When I was twelve or so I decided that was about the best way to think of Bob: he was an accident that happened to me, like getting run over by a truck, I was just in the way. I had to live with him, but like a broken leg, not like a person. I stopped trying to work out in advance what would make him happy or not or mad or not, because I never would be able to work it out, and I stopped thinking it had a whole lot to do with me. If he hit me it was like the weather, sometimes it rains, sometimes it doesn't. He didn't hit me because I was bad, like I used to think. He hit me because he could get away with it and nobody could stop him. That's mostly why people do stuff like that, because they can get away with it.

My mother was full of schemes. She was always reading

the back pages of magazines, those ads that tell you how to start your own business in your home and make thousands of dollars. She tried a lot of them too, she addressed envelopes, she sold magazine subscriptions and encyclopedias and stuff like that door to door, she even tried arts and crafts, putting together dried flower arrangements out of the raw materials they'd send to her. Once she even rented a knitting machine. That one died a quick death.

But it was no use, she never did get rich the way they promised, you'd have to work forty-eight hours a day anyway on most of those things just to break even, and she'd lose interest pretty fast. She didn't have the business sense to handle things that really would work, like Tupperware parties. Not that we lived in Tupperware country, no way she could've had one of those parties in any of our apartments, with the cat litter box in the kitchen and the lightbulbs with no shades and the red stains down the backs of the toilets and that smell, and Bob sitting there in his cardigan with the ravelly cuffs and his cigarette cough, like his insides were going to come up any minute. That and chip dip and salads with baby marshmallows in them don't mix, you know?

She was more interested in reading the ads anyway, and sending off the first letter. That always excited her. For her it was like gambling, she wanted to believe in fate, she wanted to believe that some day the wheel would come around and it would be her turn, not for anything she'd done that would make her deserve it, but just because it was her turn. She never said so, she used to say we should make the most of what we had and be thankful for our blessings, but underneath it I think she hated those cellars and the smell of cat piss and maybe even Bob as much as I did. But she didn't know what else to do, she didn't know how to get out.

Where there's life there's hope, that's what my mother would say. She had to believe good luck was out there somewhere and it was waiting for her. All those years I didn't see her I used to send her a Loto Canada or a Wintario ticket for her birthday, sometimes a book of them when I had the money, but she never won.

●

Rennie's dreaming, she knows it, she wants to wake up.

She's standing in her grandmother's garden, around at the side of the house, she knows this garden disappeared a long time ago, I can't take care of everything, said her mother, but here it is, back in place, everything is so bright, so full of juice, the red zinnias, the hollyhocks, the sunflowers, the poles with scarlet runner beans, the hummingbirds like vivid bees around them. It's winter though, there's snow on the ground, the sun is low in the sky; small icicles hang from the stems and blossoms. Her grandmother is there, in a white cotton dress with small blue flowers on it, it's a summer dress, she doesn't seem to mind the cold, and Rennie knows this is because she is dead. There's an open window, through it Rennie can hear her mother and her aunts singing hymns in the kitchen while they do the dishes, three-part harmony.

Rennie puts out her hands but she can't touch her grandmother, her hands go right in, through, it's like touching water or new snow. Her grandmother smiles at her, the hummingbirds are around her head, lighting on her hands. Life everlasting, she says.

Rennie struggles to wake up, she doesn't want to be in this dream, and finally she makes it. She's lying in her bed, the sheet's twisted around her, she thrashes and untangles herself and pushes herself upright. Outside the window it's grey, the room is dim, perhaps it's not yet morning. There's something she has to find. She stands up, in her bare feet, she's wearing a long white cotton gown, it ties at the back, but this is not a hospital. She gets to the other side of the room and pulls open her bureau drawers, one after another, rummaging through her slips, scarves, sweaters with their arms tucked carefully behind them. It's her hands she's looking for, she knows she left them here somewhere, folded neatly in a drawer, like gloves.

Rennie opens her eyes; this time she's really awake. It's dawn, the noises are beginning, the mosquito netting hangs around her in the warm air like mist. She sees where she is, she's here by herself, she's stranded in the future. She doesn't know how to get back.

●

What do you dream about? Rennie asked Jake, a month after they'd started living together.

You sound like my mother, Jake said. Next thing you'll want to know about my bowel movements.

Jake was in the habit of making Jewish-mother jokes, which Rennie felt was just a way of not really talking about his mother. She resented all jokes about mothers, even the ones she made about her own. Mothers were no laughing matter. You don't have a monopoly on mothers, she said. And I'm not yours. You should be flattered that I'm even interested.

Why does every woman in the world need to know that? said Jake. A few good fucks and they have to know what you dream. What difference does it make?

I just wanted to know you better, said Rennie. I want to know everything about you.

I'd have to be crazy to tell you anything at all, said Jake. You'd use it against me. I've seen those notebooks of yours. You'd keep lists. I bet you go through the trash can when I'm out.

Why are you so defensive? said Rennie. Don't you trust me?